'Would make fascinating reading for men too . . . *Girls Are Best* is packed with fascinating facts with which to wow friends. It is an education and a revelation, a great book to dip in and out of and to learn from'

WRITE…

'This book is … is very funny and has great facts about girls'

JADE ISSACS, 9, *THE TIMES*

'A book which will make girls realize that anything is possible – and that women have already done most of everything already!'

JULIA ECCLESHARE, *LOVEREADING*

'… funny, and full of facts that may surprise parents too'

SHEILA HANCOCK, *THE TIMES*

'The book to buy for daughters . . . lively, entertaining, illustrated snippets about the great women in history and the restrictions that they overcame, and will arm readers for arguments about gender equality'

SUNDAY TIMES

ALSO BY SANDI TOKSVIG:

Hitler's Canary
Sandi Toksvig's Guide to France
Sandi Toksvig's Guide to Spain

FOR YOUNGER READERS:

The Littlest Viking
Super-saver Mouse
Super-saver Mouse to the Rescue
The Troublesome Tooth Fairy
Unusual Day

SANDI TOKSVIG

RED FOX

GIRLS ARE BEST
A RED FOX BOOK 978 1 862 30429 1

First published in Great Britain by Doubleday,
an imprint of Random House Children's Books
A Random House Group Company

Doubleday edition published 2008
Red Fox edition published 2009

1 3 5 7 9 10 8 6 4 2

The Random House Group Limited supports the Forest Stewardship Council (FSC), the leading international forest certification organization. All our titles that are printed on Greenpeace-approved FSC-certified paper carry the FSC logo. Our paper procurement policy can be found at www.rbooks.co.uk/environment.

Set in Bell MT Regular

Interior designed by Clair Lansley

Red Fox Books are published by Random House Children's Books,
61–63 Uxbridge Road, London W5 5SA

www.**kidsatrandomhouse**.co.uk
www.**rbooks**.co.uk

Addresses for companies within The Random House Group Limited can be found at: www.randomhouse.co.uk/offices.htm

THE RANDOM HOUSE GROUP Limited Reg. No. 954009

A CIP catalogue record for this book is available from the British Library.

Printed and bound in Great Britain by
CPI Bookmarque, Croydon, CR0 4TD

DEDICATED TO THE WORK OF THE
WOMANKIND WORLDWIDE CHARITY

CONTENTS

First of all – why do we even need to show that Girls Are Best?

Well, mostly because girls are often forgotten.

History of everything

When the pilgrims landed in America, they wrote something called the Mayflower Compact. It set out the first laws of the new nation and 41 men signed it. The women who had travelled with them did not. Not even the midwife, Bridget Lee Fuller, who had delivered two babies at sea, thus actually helping to bring new life to the colonies, was allowed to put down her name.

Q. In how many countries in the world do women earn the same as men?

A. None

Too often history has seemed to be *his* story: full of a lot of men galloping about doing important things while presumably women stayed at home and made soup. The thing is (and try not to be shocked) – it's *not true.* Women have been fighting, leading, inventing, writing, painting and anything else you can think of since the beginning of time but often not getting the credit.

And it's not just the history. Sometimes we don't even know the basics . . .

Let's start with the stuff everybody knows.

Boys are bigger than girls, right?

Not if you're a Triplewart Seadevil or a Zeus Water Bug.

A what?

I see I have your attention.

The Triplewart Seadevil is great. Well, if you're a girl. It's a kind of fish. At least the females look like a fish. The boys are so small they don't look like anything much. They don't even have a digestive system. The only way for a boy Triplewart to survive is by finding a girl and clinging onto her for the rest of his life. It's a bit like a boyfriend who keeps saying, 'I'll die if you leave me' - except in this case, of course, it's true.

The Zeus Water Bug boys are so small they live in a little dip in the girl's back. How annoying would that be when you need a minute to yourself? The bug and the devil are not the only ones. There are female octupuses that are five times the size of the males, spiders so big they eat their boyfriends when they've finished with them, and female hippos who can eat a quarter of their own body weight in one go.

OK, so not all boys are bigger than girls, but they are stronger. Right?

Depends what you mean by strong.

The Olympic woman weight-lifter **Cheryl Haworth** can lift the equivalent of two fridges over her head.

THAT'S STRONG.

Usually boys *are* stronger on the outside because they turn food into

Muscle and Energy

Girls turn food into

Fat (ugh!)

But that means girls are stronger on the inside when it comes to . . .

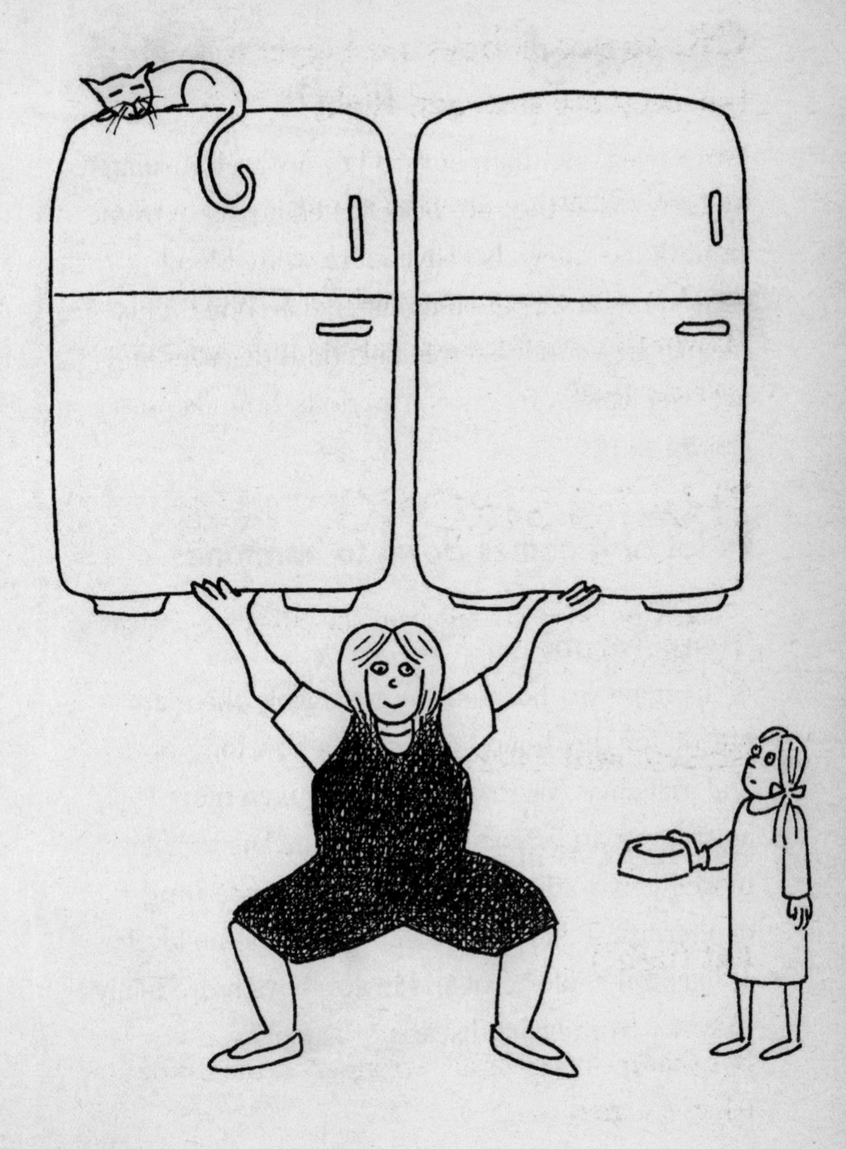

Surviving!

Girls sweat less than boys. They are well insulated by their fat so they are better at enduring extreme conditions. They also have more white blood cells and make antibodies faster than boys. This means they develop fewer infectious diseases and are usually sick for shorter periods. Sounds pretty strong to me.

A lot of it comes down to hormones

Testosterone

is the male sex hormone and probably the main reason for the difference between how long boys and girls live. Testosterone makes men more aggressive and competitive. This means they are more likely to die fighting or doing something dangerous. Testosterone also increases the levels of harmful cholesterol and makes boys more likely to suffer from heart disease or a stroke.

Oestrogen

is the female sex hormone. It lowers harmful cholesterol and raises 'good' cholesterol. It helps prevent heart disease and strokes and generally delays death.

All this means that men are actually weaker than women. Their immune systems are weaker, and their bodies are less able to process fat.

Boys may be able to lift heavy things but girls are generally fitter.

This means girls

Live longer!

Women have been living longer than men since at least the 1500s, even taking into account the risk of dying during childbirth.

Worldwide there are nine times as many women as men over 100.

Women outlive men in both rich and poor countries, often by about ten years.

Even in the animal kingdom girls can live longer. Ever see a pheasant in the road?

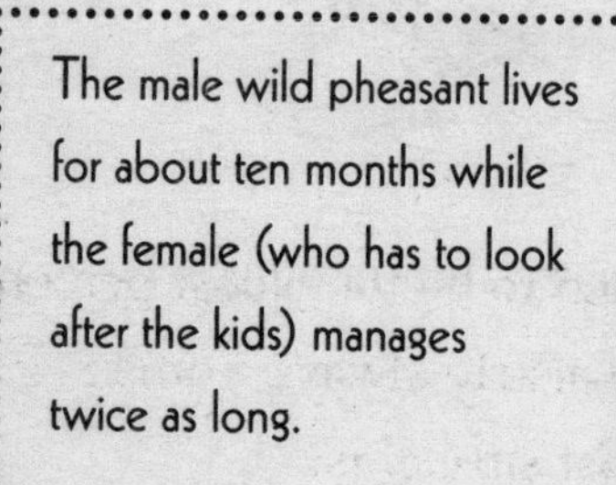

The male wild pheasant lives for about ten months while the female (who has to look after the kids) manages twice as long.

Really Old People
(Mostly Grannies)

Lots of people have claimed to be the oldest person in the world and they are nearly always women. The person we can be most sure of is:

Jeanne Calment of France (1875–1997), who was 122 years and 164 days old when she died. The odds against living that long are about six billion to one. She met the great painter Vincent Van Gogh when she was 14.

Vincent Van Gogh - self-portrait

At the moment of writing, the oldest person alive is another woman – 115-year-old American **Edna Parker**, who was born on 20 April 1893.

Varvara Semennikova from Russia died in March 2008. She is thought to have been 117 years old.

Margaret 'Peg' Wilcox Richards (1893–1999) lived to be 106. She took part in the Golden Age Games, winning gold medals in canoeing year after year. She competed from the age of 91 until she was 103. She only stopped because she couldn't see properly any more.

Oldest woman to loop the loop

Adeline Ablitt (b. 1903)

Adeline was 95 when she took to the skies in a glider and looped the loop. In her youth she was one of the first women to ride a scooter around her native Coventry. In her 90s she also took up swimming.

STRONG, FIT WOMEN

Dancing on Ice

Madge Syers (1881–1917)
Before 1902 no woman had taken part in the Ice Skating World Championships. Madge, who was British, checked the rules and realized there was nothing in them that said women couldn't take

part – it had never occurred to the International Skating Union that they would even try. Madge entered and came second. Lots of people thought she should have won, including the great Ulrich Salchow. He is said to have taken off his medal and given it to her. After that the rules were changed, banning women. The organizers claimed that their long skirts made it difficult for the judges to see their feet, so Madge began a new trend, wearing shorter skirts in everyday life.

In 1903 a new competition, the Championship of Great Britain, was launched for men *and* women. Madge won. She was the first woman ever to compete in ice skating and the first female World and Olympic Champion.

Women tennis players during Victorian times

Tennis

Billie Jean King
(1943–)
Billie Jean believed that women tennis players should be treated the same as men. A man called Bobby Riggs teased her and in 1973 challenged her to a 'battle-of-the-sexes' tennis match. He said he wanted to get women 'back into the house where they belong'. 30,000 people came to watch and more than 50 million saw it on TV. She won.

Question: Who introduced tennis to America?

Althea Gibson (1927–)

In 1950 Althea became the first African-American to compete in the US Open tennis competition. In 1951 she was the first black woman to be invited to enter the American Lawn Tennis Association Championships, and the first black person of either sex to win at Wimbledon.

Chris Evert (1954–)

In 1989 Chris became the first tennis player, boy or girl, to reach 1,000 wins.

Answer: Mary Ewing Outerbridge in 1874, after a holiday in Bermuda.

Swimming

Agnes Beckwith

In 1875, while just a teenager, Agnes swam the river Thames from London Bridge to Greenwich (about six miles). In 1880 she trod water for 30 hours in the whale tank of the Royal Aquarium of Westminster to equal the record set by Matthew Webb.

Sybil Bauer

In 1924 the boys were probably sorry they let girls swim in the Olympics. Sybil won the 100-metre backstroke in 1:23.2, which beat the men's world record.

Gertrude 'Trudy' Ederle

Trudy was from New York City, but in 1926, when she was 19, she became the first woman to swim the English Channel. She did it in 14 hours, 31 minutes, which was two hours faster than the best boy at the time.

left: Gertrude Ederle swimming the English Channel

below: Welcome party in Dover

Feats of strength

Lena Jordan

In 1897 Lena, a young Latvian, became the first person in the world to do a triple somersault on the flying trapeze. No man managed to do it till 1909.

Lillian Leitzel (1882–?)

In 1918, at the age of 36, Lillian held the world record for one-armed chin-ups. She did 27 with her right arm and then 19 with her left.

IF WOMEN CAN BE STRONG AND FIT, WHAT STOPPED THEM FROM DOING MORE THINGS?

Have a seat while I change my clothes . . .

It's hard to imagine, but one of the reasons why women in the past didn't do lots of things is because of the clothes they were supposed to wear. There was a dreadful thing called . . .

The Corset

This was an item of underwear stiffened with pieces of whale bone or metal. It laced up at the back and was pulled tight to give women tiny 15-inch waists, often causing injuries. Unable to breathe or sit or walk properly, women then had to wear huge dresses on top of the corset. It's no wonder many of them never went far from home.

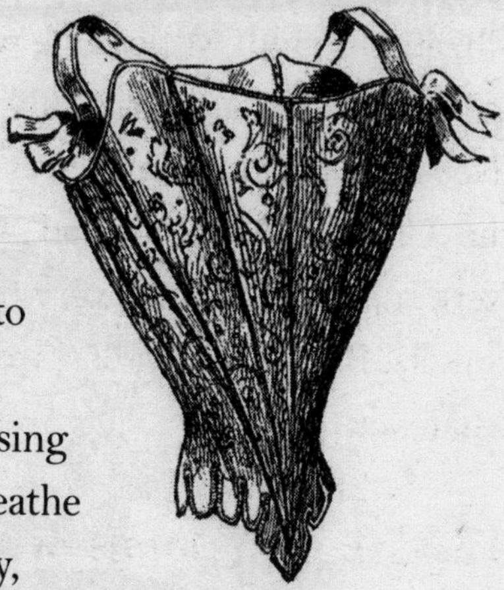

Not surprisingly, it was women themselves who put an end to all this. By changing their clothes they allowed themselves to move about more easily and soon set out on bicycles, and later in cars, to explore the world.

We should all be grateful to:
Elizabeth Smith Miller (1822–1911)

Every girl in the world should give thanks to Elizabeth Smith Miller. She was born in America in 1822 to an amazing family who risked their lives rescuing runaway slaves on what was called the 'Underground Railroad'. In those days women were supposed to wear very big dresses over tight corsets. But Elizabeth decided she wanted to wear what were known as

Turkish pantaloons or trousers

Elizabeth went to visit her cousin, Elizabeth Cady Stanton, who thought the trousers were so marvellous, she wanted some for herself.

Elizabeth Cady Stanton

THE BLOOMER COSTUME.

Mrs Stanton said: *'The question is no longer, how do you look, but woman, how do you feel?'*

She wrote:

In the spring of 1851, while spending many hours at work in the garden, I became so thoroughly disgusted with the long skirt, that the dissatisfaction - the growth of years - suddenly ripened into the decision that this shackle should no longer be endured. The resolution was at once put into practice. Turkish trousers to the ankle with a skirt reaching some four inches below the knee, were substituted for the heavy, untidy and exasperating old garment.

A friend of hers, Amelia Bloomer, wrote about this great new item of clothing in her newspaper, *The Lily*, and soon everyone was calling the trousers

'Bloomers'

SO GIRLS CAN BE STRONG AND (if they're dressed properly) GOOD AT SPORT, BUT PLEASE, BOYS ARE BEST AT FIGHTING.

Well, actually, they're not the only ones . . .

It's easy to look at history and assume that war and fighting were something that only men took part in, but check again and you will find that lots of brave women were involved in battles, sieges and duels.

Did you know that during the Second World War, 800,000 women fought in the Russian army – 560,000 of them at the front (100,000 of them received medals)? And did you know that the Soviet Union had 1,000 women fighter and military transport pilots? How about the fact that 12,000 women fought for the Israeli army in the 1948 War of Independence? The Israelis researched women's skill in combat and found that childless women were just as good or better than men. The only reason women with kids were not quite as good is that they didn't want to kill people. This shows that girls are also best at setting a good example as parents.

If you need proof that women are good at fighting, then just look at all the laws passed over the years trying to stop them . . .

Laws forbidding women to fight

AD 200 Emperor Alexander Severus banned women from fighting as gladiators.

AD 590 The synod of Druim Ceat tried to stop women from serving as soldiers but failed because the women warriors refused to give up.

1189 The Pope banned women from joining the Third Crusade. Over the years various Popes tried to stop women from engaging in martial combat or wearing armour (it was one these decrees that was used against Joan of Arc).

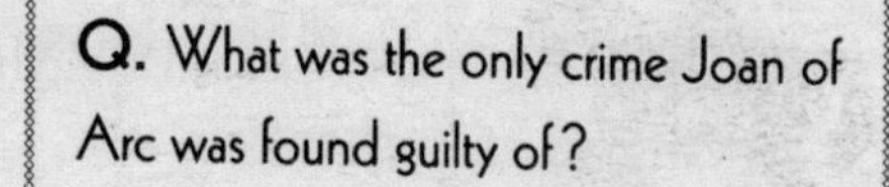

Q. What was the only crime Joan of Arc was found guilty of?

1644 King Charles I of England banned women in the English army from wearing men's clothes.

1795 The French revolutionary government ordered Frenchwomen to go home and made it illegal for them to attend political meetings or even meet in groups of five or more.

1950 David Ben Gurion ordered women in the Israeli army out of the front line (the last woman left in the mid 1960s).

A. Wearing men's clothes.

WOMEN FIGHTERS IN HISTORY

Amazons

The ancient Greeks had legendary women fighters called Amazons. They were supposed to have invented the javelin, the shield and the battle-axe.

Amazons

The **kings of Persia** are said to have had female bodyguards.

The **nizams of Hyderabad** in south-central India had female guards.

The **kings of Kandy** in Sri Lanka were protected by archeresses.

There were squads of **female cavalry** in 11th-century Japan.

Attila the Hun (450) had women serving in his army. So did **Genghis Khan** (12th century) when he invaded the West.

In the 19th century 400 women armed with spears protected the **King of Siam.**

Women Gladiators

Although you'd never know it from the movies, in Roman times there were female gladiators called gladiatrices. The Emperor Tiberius (42 BC–AD 37) had to pass a law banning senators' daughters, granddaughters and great-granddaughters from appearing as gladiators, so there must have been quite a few of them having a go.

There are mentions of female fighters under Nero, and in an early Roman novel called *Satyricon*, Petronius writes about a female 'essediarius', who is someone who fights from a kind of chariot.

Under the Emperor Domitian (AD 51–96) many more women took to fighting in the arena – some of them, it would seem, from upper-class families; girls who wanted excitement and, quite possibly, fame, just like the boys.

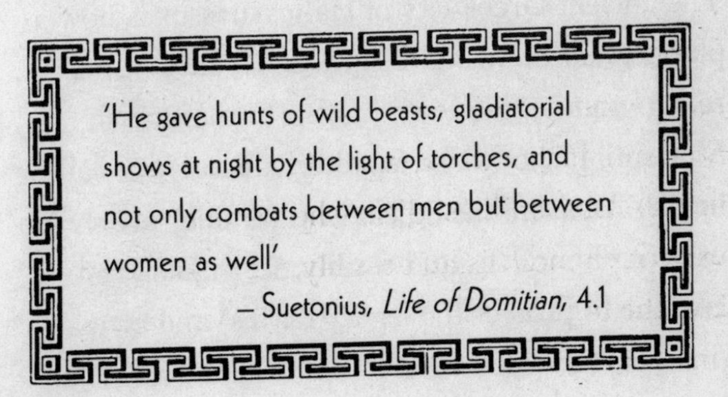

'He gave hunts of wild beasts, gladiatorial shows at night by the light of torches, and not only combats between men but between women as well'

– Suetonius, *Life of Domitian,* 4.1

Women carried on fighting professionally until AD 200, when the Emperor Severus banned girls from the arena. That doesn't mean there were no more women fighters. Lots of early writers talk about female warriors on the battlefield, and 30 captive women Goths were paraded in front of the Emperor Aurelian in AD 283.

ANYBODY WANT PROOF?

If some clever boy doesn't believe you about the female gladiators, take him to the British Museum in London and go look at

The Marble Relief from Halicarnassus

The ancient Greek city of Halicarnassus is now a place called Bodrum in Turkey. An ancient marble relief was found here and taken to the British Museum. It shows two female gladiators, one calling herself Amazon, the other Achillia. They are shown wearing loincloths and traditional gladiatorial armour to protect the legs (greaves) and arms (manica). They both carry a sword and a shield.

Q. How did the Vikings communicate at sea?

Female Vikings

Many Viking graves have revealed women buried with weapons so they clearly had women fighters. Saxon laws tried to stop women fighting – so it must have been a worry to them. A book written by Saxo Grammaticus in AD 1200 called *History of the Danes* mentions a number of Danish fighting women. He says that 'There were once women in Denmark who dressed themselves to look like men and spent almost every minute cultivating soldiers' skills.' Some of them led troops while some were 'sword maidens'. Some were members of the royalty but others were just ordinary women. There are also lots of female fighters in *The Viking Sagas*.

A. By Norse code (sorry about that).

In the eighth-century battle of Bråvalla between Sweden and Denmark, Saxo Grammaticus describes great warriors with names like Are the One-eyed, Dag the Fat and Blig Bignose, but he also mentions 300 sword maidens led by **Hed**, **Visna** and **Hedborg**. Visna had her arm cut off while carrying the Danish flag but a woman warrior called **Veborg** was said to have killed one of the champion fighters. 40,000 people died in the battle.

Pirates!

Anne Bonny

Anne Bonny (1698–1782) and **Mary Read**

Anne was born in Ireland but brought up in South Carolina in America, where her dad was a rich plantation owner. When she was 16, she married a pirate called James Bonny and her dad disowned her. Anne became a pirate in the Caribbean and then ran off with another pirate called 'Calico Jack'. She joined his crew dressed as a man and soon her fighting skill brought her plenty of plunder.

Mary was another woman disguised as a man on Calico Jack's ship. Jack became suspicious when Anne spent so much time with 'him', so Anne had to explain that Mary was also a woman. Eventually Mary and Anne were both arrested;

Q. How much did the pirate pay for his peg leg and hook?

Mary died in prison but Anne was rescued by her father. She is said to have gone on to marry a man in South Carolina, have eight children and die a respectable woman at the age of 84.

There are lots of other women pirates, like

Cheng I Sao (1775–1844)

The Chinese Cheng married a sea robber. Together she and her husband ran a group of pirates that eventually numbered over 50,000. In 1807 her husband died and Cheng I Sao took command. She was very harsh – anyone who disobeyed or stole from her was beheaded, deserters lost their ears and captives could either join up or suffer an excruciating death. The Chinese Imperial Navy tried to stop her,

A. An arm and a leg.

but by 1808 her pirates had sunk 63 navy vessels. Everyone was terrified of her. One admiral killed himself rather than be taken captive. Towards the end of her life she negotiated an amnesty with the government, retired and ran a gambling house.

Lady Mary Killigrew (active 1530–1570)
Lady Killigrew was the daughter of a Suffolk pirate. Her husband was often away and, perhaps because she was bored, Mary took to piracy. In 1583 a German merchant ship was driven into Falmouth by storms. Lady Killigrew led a boarding party, killed the crew and seized jewels, heavy silver and coins. Queen Elizabeth I, who thought the money should have been hers, was furious and had Lady Killigrew arrested. Found guilty of piracy and sentenced to hang, she was later given a jail sentence instead.

Queen Elizabeth I

Great Women Warriors

Tomoe Gozen (c.1161–c.1184)

Tomoe was one of the great female warrior samurai in Japanese history. She fought in the Genpei War. She was beautiful, brave and brilliant at riding, archery, kenjutsu and wielding the naginata pole. Tomoe fought alongside her husband in all his battles.

Princess Khutulun (c.1251–?)

Khutulun was the niece of Kublai Khan, a famous Mongol military leader who ruled parts of the world that today include China, Mongolia, Tibet, Kazakhstan, Kyrgyzstan and Turkmenistan. She loved to fight and was a legendary soldier.

According to the great explorer Marco Polo, she was stronger than any of the men in Khan's army.

It was said that she would wrestle any man who wanted to marry her. If he lost, he had to give her 100 horses; she ended up with 10,000 horses and never married.

Chief Pine Leaf (c.1806–1858)
The American Pine Leaf was born into the Gros Ventre tribe but captured and adopted by the Crow tribe when she was about ten. She always liked fighting and was recognized as a fine warrior. She single-handedly defeated an ambush by Blackfoot Indians and went on to lead several raids against them, collecting many scalps. She became an important member of the Council of Chiefs. White traders called her the Absaroka Amazon. Sadly she was killed by her own tribe.

Lilliard

In 1545, when the Earl of Arran was in charge of Scotland, Henry VIII sent 5,000 English soldiers to seize some land.

Even though the Scots had a much smaller army, they defeated the English in the Battle of Ancrum at a place called Lilliard Edge. The Edge was named after a young woman named Lilliard who fought on the Scottish side. It is said that she became enraged when her lover was slain by the English and began killing like a demon. Part of her grave can still be seen near the border between the parishes of Maxton and Ancrum. The inscription that used to be on the tombstone gives you some idea of just how angry she must have been:

FAIR MAIDEN LILLIARD LIES
UNDER THIS STANE

LITTLE WAS HER STATURE,
BUT MUCKLE WAS HER FAME;

UPON THE ENGLISH LOONS
SHE LAID MONY THUMPS

AND WHEN HER LEGS WERE
CUTTIT OFF, SHE FOUGHT
UPON HER STUMPS

Queen Vishpla (thousands of years ago)
Vishpla was a game girl. A book called the *Rig-Veda*, which was written in India somewhere between 3,500 and 1,800 BC, tells how Queen Vishpla was wounded while leading her troops into battle and had her leg amputated. Once the wound had healed, she was fitted with an iron leg, enabling her not just to walk but to go back into battle. She was the first person known to have an artificial leg, which is an odd kind of fame.

Dressing up as men in order to fight

Kit Cavanagh (?–1739)
Kit started her military career in the 1690s, disguised as a man. She originally joined the army to look for her husband but fought bravely in the Scots Greys. Her true sex was discovered when she was wounded in battle but she continued to fight as a woman. She died of natural causes and

is one of only two women buried with military honours at Chelsea Hospital in London.

Catalina de Erauso, the Lieutenant Nun

(1592–1650)

Catalina fought as a man, but started out as a nun. She was born in Spain and when she was four, her parents put her into the convent of San Sebastian el Antiguo. Catalina hated it.

The day before she was due to take her vows she ran away, dressed as a man, and joined the Spanish army to fight in the New World. She became a second lieutenant, even taking command when her captain was killed, and was known to her fellow soldiers as 'Alferez'. Her real sex was revealed when she was captured. The penalty for dressing as a man was death, but she petitioned the king and was granted mercy. She then returned to Spain and spent the rest of her life working as a muleteer under the name Antonio de Erauso. She continued to wear men's clothes till she died and always carried a sword and dagger decorated with silver.

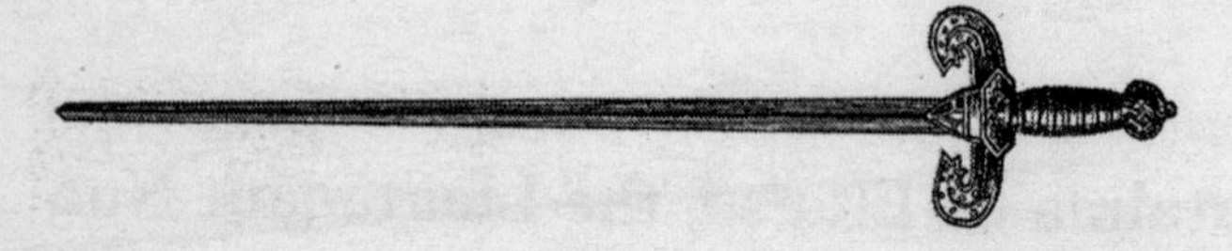

But all that was a long time ago, wasn't it? I mean, it wouldn't be like that now, would it?

Well, how about the Second World War?

The Night Witches

The nickname of the Second World War Soviet 588th Night Bomber Regiment. This was one of three women-only Russian air regiments. There were over 800,000 Russian women in military service and the women's air regiments flew over 30,000 missions.

Still not recent enough?

Gaddafi's Amazons

Colonel Muammar Gaddafi is the leader of the North African country of Libya. He uses 30 highly trained women as his personal bodyguard.

All right, all right – girls are strong and brave – but boys are cleverer than girls, right?

Aren't they? I mean, historically they've achieved more – invented more things, written more books and music . . .

Hmm!

Sorry – that was an empty space because I needed to cough for a minute.

Let's take a look at the brain, shall we?

(You may want to wear trainers as it could be slippery . . .)

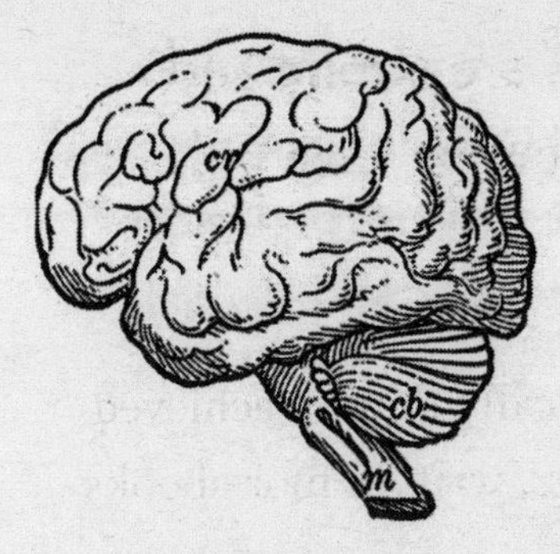

Fact: Male brains are about 10 per cent larger than women's.

Reality: This does not necessarily make them 10 per cent smarter.

It's not how much brain you have, it's how you use it – size does not matter! Let's start by looking at how information gets into the brain:

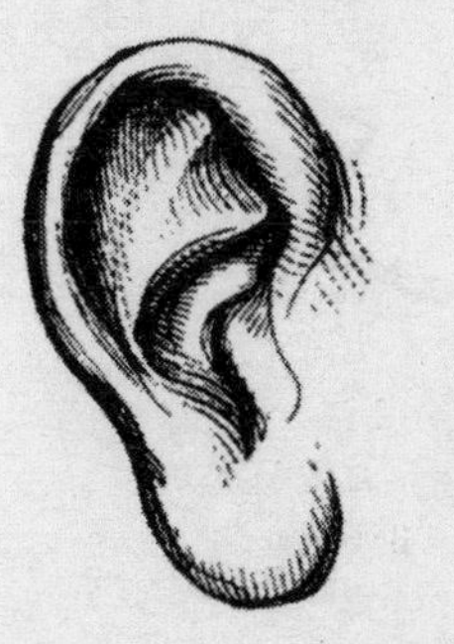

'Friends, Romans,
Countrymen,
lend me your
ears . . .'

Q. According to the UN, what percentage of the world's work is done by women?

A. 75 per cent.

Listening

When boys listen, they only use one small part of the brain. When girls listen, they use both sides of the brain. This means that girls are better at following instructions.

Hello? Is anybody there?

Listening for a living

When the telephone was first introduced (around 1878), all calls had to be put through a large switchboard by an operator. The work was very complicated. Each operator watched over as many as 200 phone lines. They were expected to answer a call within four seconds, handle up to 600 calls an hour, be polite, and also be ready with information about travel, the weather and anything else the customer wanted. At first the telephone companies hired boys, but the boys were rude, cut people off and didn't pay attention. The bosses soon realized they needed to hire women. Women were patient and good listeners. By 1900, almost all operators were women.

The women were brilliant workers but they were badly paid and the job was barred to those who were married or black or Jewish.

Yeah, but boys' brains are still bigger! Still thinking about size? OK.

The Neuron Numbers Game

The brain is made up of cells called neurons. Girls' brains have more neurons. They have smaller brains but they are made up of more of the good stuff.

What does that mean?

When you compare the intelligence of boys and girls, they score about the same, but girls score higher on being able to think in a versatile way. This means that girls can make quick decisions without seeming to think about it. Some people call this 'women's intuition'. Let's imagine how this might work if you were in space.

You're in space and a meteor comes hurtling towards you.

'Oh no, here comes a meteor!'

A boy will: think logically about the best course of action. He will think:

He will try to turn the spaceship. By the time he has thought all this, the meteor will have hit him.

A girl will: not appear to think at all but instinctively turn the spaceship and save herself.

Q. So if women can deal with meteors so well, why aren't there more women astronauts?

WARNING – THE REASON IS REALLY SILLY AND MAY MAKE YOU CROSS.

Suits you, sir.

A. The reason why there have been so few women astronauts is because the spacesuits are the wrong size.

What?

In the 1990s the American space agency decided to get some new spacesuits. They only ordered them in medium and large because that covered most astronauts. The agency decided it wasn't worth buying suits for a few small men or for women. Mary Ellen Weber, a former astronaut, trained for a spacewalk but never did one. She commented, 'I think it's a mistake to make equipment decisions that eliminate almost half of the population from participating in an activity.' The lack of small spacesuits means that NASA can't find out how good women might be in space.

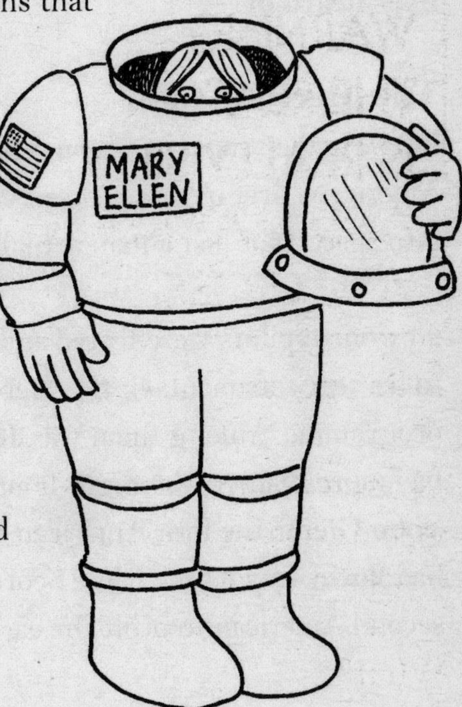

Q. Of the 157 NASA astronauts who have walked in space, how many have been women?

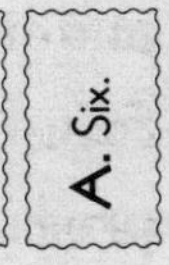

A QUICK BIT OF EXTRA HISTORY

Ever heard of

The Mercury 13?

In 1958 (the year I was born, so a fine year) the Americans first began to research putting a man into space. Not just a man actually.

25 women pilots were tested and 13 were chosen to become astronauts in the Mercury space programme. Among them was **Jerrie Cobb**, who had more than 10,000 flight hours to her name. (John Glenn, the first American to orbit the earth, had flown only 5,000, while Scott Carpenter, the second American to orbit the earth, had 2,900.)

Jerrie went through the same tests as the men and her results were fantastic. Suddenly, in July 1961, NASA cancelled the women's space programme. When asked why, they said it was because the women had never gone through the jet-aircraft testing. The reason why they hadn't? They weren't allowed to until 1973.

Multi-tasking –
or rubbing your
stomach and
patting your
head at
the same
time.

Apart from having more neurons, girls tend to use more parts of their brain to get things done. This may explain why women often recover better after suffering a stroke. (This is when the brain is damaged because of losing blood supply.) Women are able to use other parts of the brain to take over from the injured areas. Some people think the *corpus callosum* (the bit that connects the two halves of the brain) is thicker in women so the two halves can work together more easily but no one knows that for sure. What we do know is that Girls Are Best at what's called

multi-tasking

or doing several things at once.

Quick Q. What percentage of the world's assets are owned by women?

A. 1 per cent.

The Great Supermarket Race

Try this test the next time you are in a supermarket with someone else. Each of you joins a queue the same length – one with a man on the till and one with a woman. See who gets through first. It will most likely be the one queuing for the woman's till because women are better at the multi-tasking needed for this kind of work.

NOTE: This does not make either working in, or going to, the supermarket any more fun.

So girls have better brains which they use better, but what do they use them for?

Back to the old brain again. The left side of the brain is the bit that generally deals with language. This half develops faster in girls than in boys. By the age of 12 girls are about four years ahead of boys in language skills. There used to be a test for kids called the '11 plus' which had some problems that needed to be solved by using language. The test had to be changed to bring boys' scores up to the level of the girls'.

Oh dear, I'm starting to feel bad for the boys. Quick – boys' brains make them very good at . . .

Map reading

Boys are good at reading maps. This is that hormone testosterone again. Testosterone seems to help that part of the brain that makes you good at things like map reading. For girls there is sat nav and asking directions.

Boys have testosterone, girls have oestrogen, right?

So can't oestrogen map read?

No, but it is the hormone that helps develop the part of the brain used to remember things. (It's called the hippocampus, which sounds like a place where hippos go to get a degree.) So while boys in the womb are busy improving their map-reading skills, girls are preparing to remember how to get somewhere in the first place. Girls have better memories. They remember where things are and notice if anything changes.

Oestrogen also helps to activate the bit of the brain that recognizes smell so **girls' noses are great at sniffing** things out.

The Memory Game

Try this with boys and girls and see who does best. Girls tend to be better at remembering where things are.

Cover the picture below with a piece of paper. Give everyone a chance to look at the objects on the opposite page for a minute. Then cover that page and uncover this one. Give everyone a minute to decide what is missing.

Note: more than one item is missing!

Where are my trainers?

If you are looking for something in the house, you'll probably ask your mum rather than your dad. He'll say he can find it but she will actually do so.

A study at the University of Florida showed that men are sure they can find things but often can't (they have more confidence than skill), while women aren't sure they can find things but will (more skill than confidence).

WARNING:

I'm going to get emotional in a minute, so skip this bit if you can't bear that.

Girls are cry babies

True, and a good thing too.

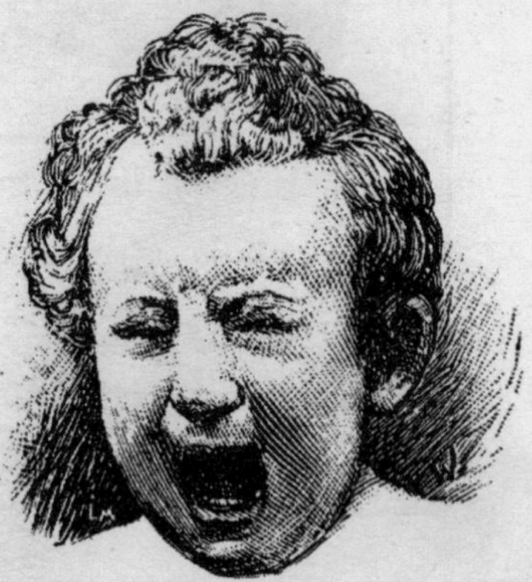

There are lots of books that tell you how great boys are. Boys are really good at figuring out how things work. Girls reckon that is what instruction booklets are for and don't worry about it.

Girls are better at emotion. Being good at emotion means you will be better at dealing with other people. Basically boys like to find out how things work while girls like to find out how *people* work. Boys and girls have different ways of dealing with emotion because of the

amygdala

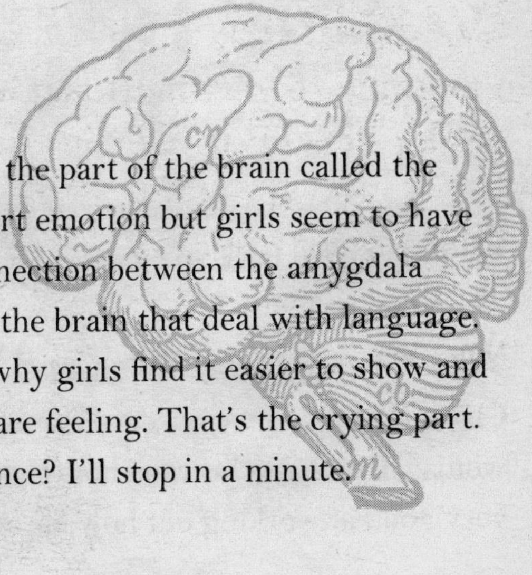

Both sexes use the part of the brain called the amygdala to sort emotion but girls seem to have a stronger connection between the amygdala and the bits of the brain that deal with language. Maybe this is why girls find it easier to show and say what they are feeling. That's the crying part. Too much science? I'll stop in a minute.

There is also a chemical reason for women being better at emotion. Women produce more *Oxytocin*. This is a brain chemical designed to help mothers want to look after their babies. It makes women more in tune with emotion.

Boys' and girls' brains are wired differently – I think it started back when everyone lived in caves.

Your Average Cave Man and Woman

Cro and Magnon were a cave man and cave woman. Cro spent his time hunting and became very good at working out how far away a potential dinner was. This made his vision rather narrow and focused. He would run around on his own and wasn't very good at seeing how other people were doing. Because Magnon had children she couldn't go hunting. (This is a story you will hear again and again.) She stayed home with the kids, waiting for Cro. Sometimes Cro took a long time to come back with food and the kids started crying because they were hungry. So Magnon strapped them to her back and went looking for food. This job

involved looking around to see what was growing. At the same time she had to make sure the kids were OK. She became very good at having a wide vision and living in a group with the other mothers and kids. They all needed to get on so she became good at checking other people's emotions.

So girls are emotional and boys always think clearly?

Uh, not exactly.

They say that the way to a man's heart is through his stomach. Well, now science has proved it is true.

A study in *The British Journal of Psychology* in 2007 showed that the kind of woman a man fancies depends on how hungry he is. The study proved that when men are hungry, they find bigger women more attractive. Hungry men pay less attention to the shape of a woman's body.

Apparently it goes back to times when food was scarce; heavier women looked healthier than those who were skinny. Hungry men think with their stomachs.

So here is the
BIG question –
if girls' brains
are so good, why
aren't there more
of them in the lists
of great writers
and thinkers?

Hmm. Don't seem to be many black or Asian people either. There are an awful lot of white boys in history. You don't think it could be to do with opportunity, do you?

Up until about 50 years ago lots of people thought women weren't as clever as men. Even brilliant men like Charles Darwin, who came up with the theory of evolution, thought that women were born less clever. Then other people began to study men and women and realized that it isn't a question of how big your brain is but whether you get a chance in life.

One of the problems that faced girls is that for years and years they weren't allowed to go to school.

Hurray! No School!

Well, it might be fun for a day or two, but after that I should think it would be boring. Imagine never learning how to read.

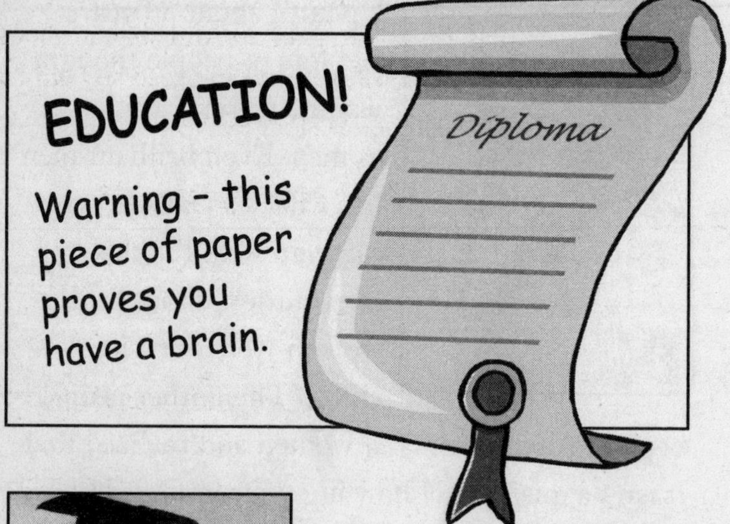

Quick Q. When did Cambridge University let women graduate?

A. Not until after the Second World War.

Reading (not the town in Berkshire)

In every country where boys and girls get the same education, girls do better at reading than boys. Sadly there are still lots of places where girls aren't taught to read. Worldwide, fewer girls go to school than boys, so fewer girls are able to read. In Afghanistan about 87 per cent of women can't read and only 30 per cent of girls go to school.

Fighting to go to school!

Lots of girls in the past wanted to go to school and use their brains. There were plenty of clever girls. Take

Elena Lucrezia Cornaro Piscopia

(1646–1684)

Elena was born in Venice to a noble family. She loved learning. Women didn't go to university so she studied at home. In 1677 she asked the University of Padua if they would test her even though she had never been to a single lecture. She was examined for a doctorate in philosophy and got her degree in 1678, making her the first woman ever to graduate from a university.

Pretending to be a boy to get to study

Agnodike (last third of the 4th century BC)
Agnodike wanted to study medicine in Athens, but girls were barred from doing so. In the end she disguised herself as a man and was taught by Herophilus, one of the founders of the scientific method of medicine. She studied because she wanted to help sick women, but when she finished, the women wouldn't let her treat them because they thought she was a man. She confessed that she was actually a woman, but was then arrested for breaking the law. Fortunately the judge, Areopagus, realized she was trying to do good and decided to rewrite the law, allowing women to practise medicine and to be paid. Because of brave women like Agnodike there are now women doctors all over the world.

Q. Until 1944 what did British women teachers have to do when they got married?

A. Give up work.

Miranda Stuart or Dr James Barry

(c.1799–1865)

Miranda first dressed as a man in 1809 so that she could get into Edinburgh University. She graduated in medicine and joined the British army, where she served for 45 years without anyone guessing that she was a woman. She worked in South Africa, the Caribbean and elsewhere, becoming recognized as a brilliant surgeon. Her secret was only discovered after she died. Must have been quite a shock for the funeral parlour.

Sophie Germain (1776–1831)
Sophie loved maths but it was not considered a suitable subject for a woman. She wanted to study with a teacher called Joseph-Louis Lagrange, so she sent him work signed 'Monsieur Le Blanc'. Lagrange was so impressed by the paper that he asked to meet Le Blanc, and she had to tell him she was a woman. He realized how clever she was and began to teach her.

In 1816 she won a mathematics competition and became the first female to attend sessions at the French Academy of Sciences. She made contributions to maths which are still important today.

$25 + 37 =$

If it was hard for white women to study, it was even harder for black women . . .

Rebecca Lee Crumpler

(1831–1895)

Rebecca was born in Delaware in America, where she was brought up by an aunt who spent much of her time caring for the sick. In 1852 Rebecca moved to Charlestown, Massachusetts, where, without any formal training, she became a nurse (the first school for nursing didn't open until 1873). In 1860 she won a place at the New England Female Medical College, and four years later became the first African-American woman in the United States to be awarded a medical degree.

In 1865 the American Civil War ended and Rebecca moved to Richmond, Virginia. Here she worked with other (male) black doctors to care for freed slaves. She concluded her life in Boston, where she treated anyone whether they could pay her or not. In 1883 Rebecca published her *Book of Medical Discourses*, one of the very first medical publications by an African American.

Yes, it's time for a quick

groan

TEST.

> If you don't like exams, blame the Chinese men who first created them in 587, or the Cambridge University Professors (all boys) who, in 1792, gave the first written exam in Europe so they could make some more money.

Here are the questions:

1. What is the name of the Olympic woman weightlifter who can lift the equivalent of two fridges above her head?
2. Who was the first person in the world to do a triple somersault on the flying trapeze?
3. Which modern head of state has an all-female bodyguard?
4. What's the bit of the brain that deals with emotion?
5. What do hungry men think with?

Are you cheating?

1. Cheryl Haworth 2. Lena Jordan
3. Colonel Gaddafi 4. The amygdala
5. Their stomachs

So did women not do anything until they went to school?

Of course they did. You know why? Because . . .

Women have been inventing things for years:

Mary Andersen – the car windscreen wiper

Melitta Bentz – coffee filter paper (OK, she may not be important to you, but I love her)

Ada Augusta Lovelace – the groundwork for developing the computer

Phyllis Pearsall – the *A–Z* maps

Jeanne Villepreux-Power – the aquarium

Stephanie Kwolek – Kevlar, used in bullet-proof vests and car tyres

Grace Hopper – the first technical program to translate English into instructions a computer can understand; she also found the first computer bug (it was a moth!)

Marion Donovan – the disposable nappy

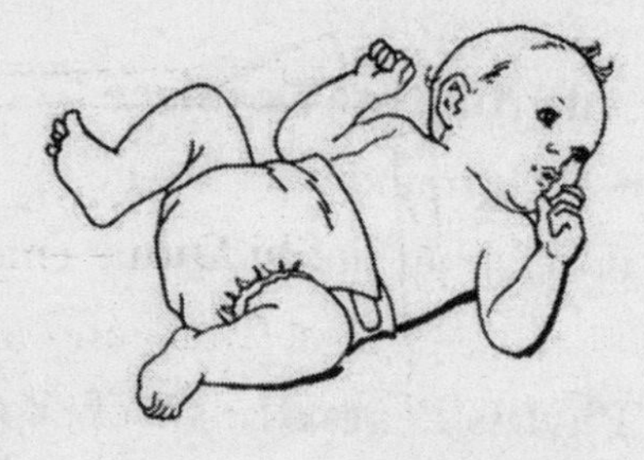

Marie Curie – the first woman to get a Nobel Prize: she discovered radioactive elements

Gertrude B. Elion – the first treatment for leukaemia, drugs for gout, malaria, meningitis, septicaemia and bacterial infections; she was awarded the Nobel Prize for medicine.

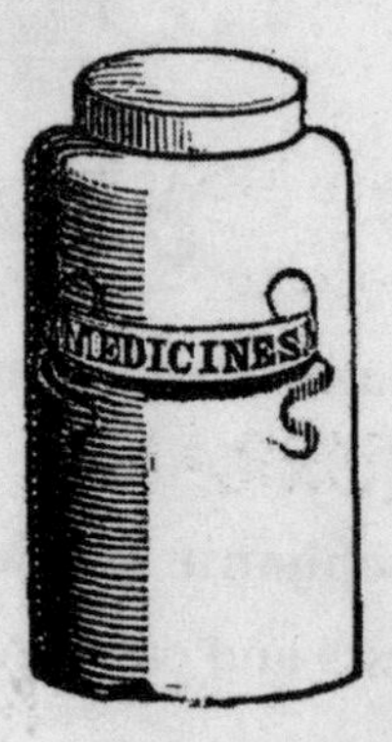

Erna Schneider Hoover – a computerized telephone switching system that helped stop overloading switchboards; the principles of her system are still used today

Shi Dun – empress of China and inventor of paper

Martha Coston – a night signal system for the American navy

Ruth Wakefield – the chocolate chip cookie

HURRAH!

Or how about some big stuff like

Agriculture?

No one can know for sure who came up with the idea of growing food in fields but let's look at the basics. Boys will tell you that they were once great hunters chasing things with spears. So if they were out hunting, they can't have had the time or the patience to make things grow slowly. It must have been the women, who were at home with the children.

The Romans thought agriculture was invented by

Ceres

Ceres was the Roman goddess of agriculture and it is from her name that we get the word 'cereal'. She gave the world corn, without which there would be a lot less breakfast cereal.

The Egyptians thought it was

Isis

Isis was an Egyptian goddess but her name written in hieroglyphs means 'human female' so she probably represented real women who had ruled in the past. The Egyptians believed that she started agriculture and invented bread-making, both of which are very important. She also invented the art of embalming (making mummies), which is less thrilling.

The Greeks thought it was

Demeter

Demeter's name means 'mother-earth' and she was, amongst other things, the Greek goddess of grain and agriculture. She first gets a mention around the seventh century BC and was worshipped all over the Greek world for having taught humans everything to do with growing food – sowing seeds, ploughing, harvesting, etc. Because of this she was especially popular with people who lived in the country.

Q. How much of the food on earth is produced by women today?

A. 80 per cent.

GETTING THE CREDIT

Any idea what this is?

It's a machine called a **cotton gin**, which sounds like a drink you could put in the washing machine. It looks unlikely, but this machine changed American history.

Back when America was a British colony, cotton was very important. It made the colonies a lot of money but was very hard to produce: it took a slave one day to separate a pound of cotton from the seed. The cotton gin sped things up so that 300 pounds a day could be cleaned. It was amazing. The president of the United States, Abraham Lincoln, said, '*How could such a simple invention alter American history in such a king-sized way?*'

American schoolchildren are taught that the cotton gin was invented by a man called **Eli Whitney** but everyone forgets about . . .

Catherine Littlefield Greene

(1755–1814)

Catherine, or Caty, as she was known, had a tough time in her early married life. First her husband was at war, then they became very poor and eventually he died. Caty was determined to support her five kids. Eli Whitney was tutoring her neighbour's children and she gave him a room at her farm. Caty watched the workers in the fields and came up with an idea for a cotton machine.

She asked Eli to have a go at building it. His first attempt didn't quite work – there was a problem with the wooden teeth – and he was ready to give up. Caty suggested he use wire instead, and within ten days he had made a small working model that was the basis for all future gins. Why didn't Catherine take out the patent in her own name? It was, after all, her idea. Well, it just wasn't done.

FOOD, GLORIOUS FOOD

So women came up with the idea of growing things. But who made it into something edible?

Recipes

Invented by women, handed down from woman to woman, but we often don't have their names. These days there are hundreds of recipe books but there is still no one more famous for writing about British cooking than . . .

Isabella Mary Beeton

(1836–1865)

Isabella is always remembered as Mrs Beeton, who wrote *Mrs Beeton's Book of Household Management*, which is still used by lots of people. This book was the first to print recipes the way we are used to seeing them today. Ask your mum or your granny if they have a copy.

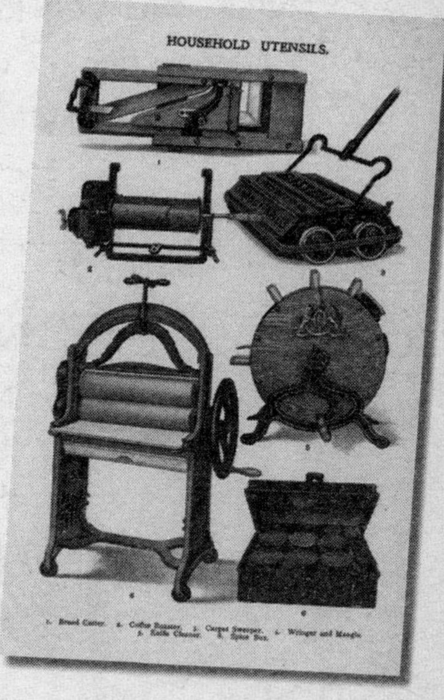

A page from Mrs Beeton's Book of Household Management

Ilustrations from Mrs Beeton's Book of Household Management

A quick 'did-you-know?' question:

Did you know that the word 'bridal' comes from beer for a bride – **bride ale**?

Beer was probably invented by women as it has a lot in common with bread-making. In medieval times, brides sold ale or beer on their wedding day to help pay for everything. This was known as 'bride-ale', which eventually became the word 'bridal' that we still use at weddings but no longer connect with beer. Women obviously liked the stuff. Ladies-in-waiting at the court of Henry VII were allowed a gallon of beer just for breakfast, and whenever she travelled,

Queen Elizabeth I sent couriers ahead to taste the local beer. If it wasn't good enough she had some sent to her from London.

And let's not forget:

Siris – goddess of beer in Mesopotamia, where beer was first made 8,000 years ago

Nimkasi – goddess of beer in ancient Sumeria, where the first recipe for beer was written down 6,000 years ago

St Brigid – a holy Irish woman who about 1,500 years ago changed poor people's bath water into beer

Nice trick.

So what do girls do with all this inventiveness?

TIME TO BE CREATIVE!

You can doodle here:

The ancient Greeks believed all art came from

The Muses

According to the Greeks, there were nine goddesses called the Muses, who were in charge of all art. They were the daughters of Zeus, king of the gods, and Mnemosyne, goddess of memory. Their names were not ones you hear every day in the playground so it was a good thing their mother was great at remembering things.

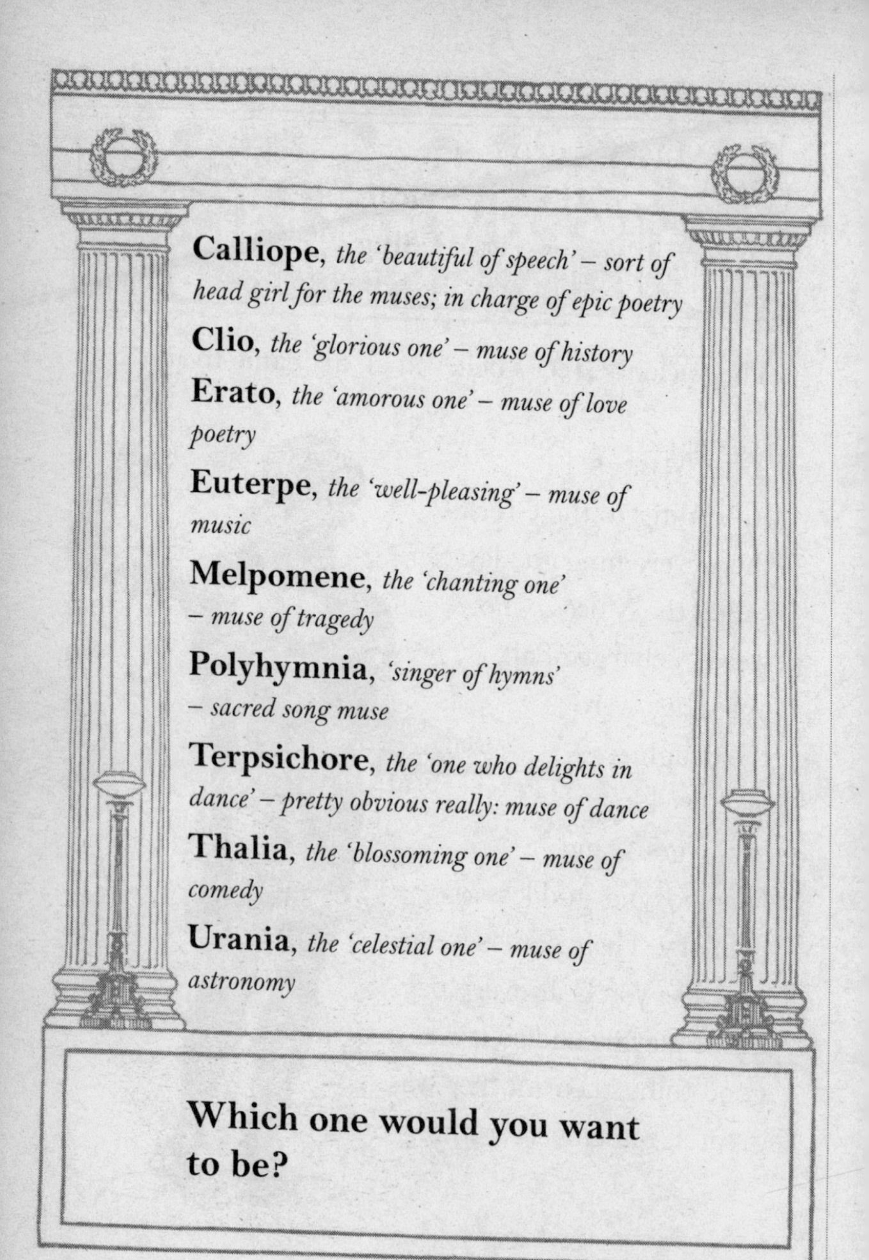

Calliope, *the 'beautiful of speech' – sort of head girl for the muses; in charge of epic poetry*

Clio, *the 'glorious one' – muse of history*

Erato, *the 'amorous one' – muse of love poetry*

Euterpe, *the 'well-pleasing' – muse of music*

Melpomene, *the 'chanting one' – muse of tragedy*

Polyhymnia, *'singer of hymns' – sacred song muse*

Terpsichore, *the 'one who delights in dance' – pretty obvious really: muse of dance*

Thalia, *the 'blossoming one' – muse of comedy*

Urania, *the 'celestial one' – muse of astronomy*

Which one would you want to be?

The Muses were

MUSical
aMUSing
had MUSEums

And they . . . .

Dropped all the ideas for art onto human heads

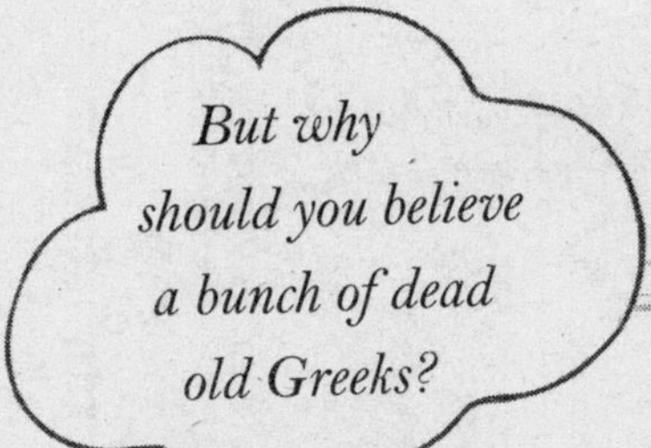

But why should you believe a bunch of dead old Greeks?

All right. How about the **Hindus** or **Buddhists**? They believed there were female spirits or nymphs called Apsaras, who were in charge of all art.

They had quite a racy dress sense.

If lots of people believed women inspired art, how come there were so many more male artists than female?

You're not making this easy for me, are you?

Sssh! It's to do with naked bodies and boys' clubs!

The trouble with nakedness

There was a lot of art created during a time in history called

The Renaissance

Well, there was a lot of art created by men. Actually, there was a lot of art created by white men. One of the big problems for women painters back then was that they weren't allowed to study the naked body.

WARNING: naked body coming up

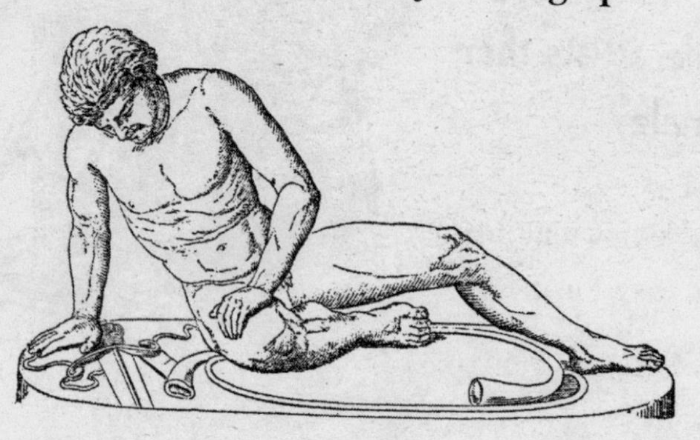

Any painter who wanted to do a big famous religious painting had to be able to draw naked men, and women were barred from doing that. They were not allowed to be in a room with nude male models so they didn't know how to paint them. No naked men – no big commissions for great big famous paintings.

The Boys' Clubs

In the 18th century lots of European countries had academies which artists needed to belong to if they wanted to get on. The academies first helped train you and then sold your work. Most of them were not open to women. The French Academy, for example, admitted a handful of women in the 1700s, but towards the end of the century decided not to accept any more.

In 1768 **Angelica Kauffmann** and **Mary Moser** helped found the Royal Academy of Arts in London, but when a portrait was done of the founders only the men of the Academy were shown gathered in a large art studio. Angelica and Mary weren't allowed to be there; their faces appeared as portraits on the wall. There were no more full female members of the Academy until 168 years later in 1936.

Angelica Kauffmann

So how did women become artists back then?

It helped if your dad was a painter

A painter probably had his own workshop, and if he was nice, he might even let a daughter use it. There were lots of women who trained in their father's footsteps.

Check out:

Artemisia Gentileschi was born in Italy in 1593. She was trained by her father, Orazio Gentileschi, and worked alongside him. She turned out to be much better at art than her brothers but wasn't allowed to join the art academies. She decided to paint naked women and lots of people were very shocked by her work. Today she is considered to be one of the best artists of her time.

BE A NUN

Being a nun in the old days wasn't all like *The Sound of Music*, but lots of women who weren't religious became nuns anyway. Why? Because for hundreds of years one of the few places where a woman could get an education was in a convent. Imagine – a nun didn't have to run a house, look after kids or make sure her husband did well at his work. She might have to wear clothes that weren't very flattering but she could get on with her painting. Over the years women painters were able to do their work because they were nuns. Women like

Q. What do you call a sleep-walking nun?

A. A roamin' Catholic.

Caterina de Virgi

Caterina was born in Italy in 1413. She became a nun when she was 14. She must have been very good at painting because she is now the patron saint of art.

Antonia Uccello

Antonia's dad was a 15th-century painter. She was a Carmelite nun hailed as 'a daughter who knew how to draw'. Lots of her dad's work is around but we don't see any of hers.

Great Women Artists You Should Know About

Sofonisba Anguissola

(c.1532–1625)

The first successful female painter of the Renaissance, she was a friend of Michelangelo, who thought she was brilliant. Sofonisba had four sisters who were also artists – two gave up when they had kids, one became a nun and one died young.

Sofonisba Anguissola

Mary Beale (1633–1699)

I really like Mary Beale. She lived in the 17th century and was probably the first professional female English painter. Mary painted for fun but when her husband Charles lost his job, she began to take her art more seriously. Charles worked as her assistant, mixing the paint and doing her accounts. If you are in London, she is buried at St James's, Piccadilly.

Making a big impression

Berthe Morisot (1841–1895)

Artists like Renoir, Sisley, Degas, Monet and Cézanne are famous for a kind of art called impressionism.

A Berthe Morisot etching

Their first Impressionist Exhibition in 1874 displayed works by 29 artists. Berthe Morisot was the only woman painter.

Berthe Morisot and daughter

Mary Cassatt (1844–1926)
Mary was born in Pennsylvania in America. She was another impressionist. Painters like Degas thought she was brilliant and she became very famous. By 1914 she was almost blind but still managed to paint 18 canvases for an exhibition to support women seeking the right to vote. Today her paintings sell for millions.

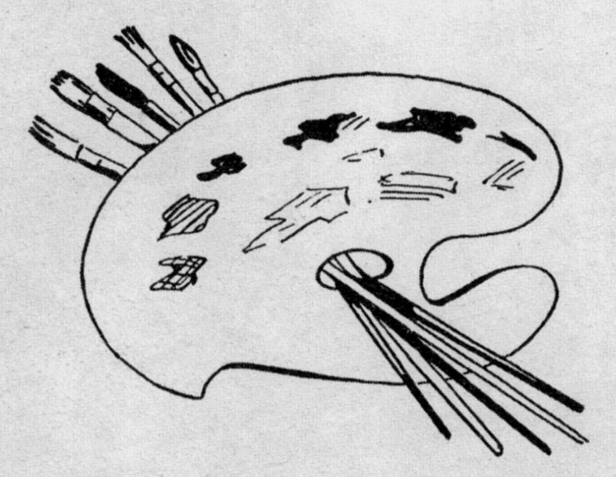

Make sure you check out an artist called **Georgia O'Keefe**. She's amazing!

Can you sign your name here?

____

What's your name?

During the Renaissance art was often created in workshops where lots of artists worked for one master. He was the one who signed the art, but that didn't mean he had created it. Women worked for these masters too but weren't allowed to hold official jobs and never signed anything. Anyway, the whole name thing can be misleading as all women used to take their husbands' last names. You probably have your dad's last name and not your mother's. If you could choose, which would you prefer?

The problem with signatures

A lot of the art created by women hasn't been signed – embroidery, jewellery, baskets and pots. You can still see this today if you go to the islands of Murano and Burano near Venice in Italy. Murano is famous for glass blowing. If you buy a piece of glass made by one of the Muranese men, you will be given a leaflet showing his face, his name and photographs of him making the glass. Burano is famous for its lace, which is made using seven different stitches. All the lace makers are women and each woman specializes in only one stitch, so it takes seven women to make one piece of Burano lace. All that work and you will never discover the name of a single one of them.

The Bayeux Tapestry

This famous tapestry is 70 metres long; it is embroidered with wool and is one of the most famous pieces of sewing in the world. It tells the story of the Battle of Hastings and the Norman Conquest of England in 1066. It was probably made by a rich lady and her servants but we don't know any of their names.

HAROLD: REX: INTERFEC
TVS: EST
HIC PORTATVR: CORPVS: EADWARDI: REGIS: AD: ECCLESIAM: SCI
PETRI APL

WOMEN AS INSPIRATION

Perhaps the most famous painting in the world is by Leonardo da Vinci. It is known as the *Mona Lisa* but is actually a portrait of Lisa Gherardini del Giocondo. She had five kids and probably didn't have time to paint herself.

Q. How many people visit the Mona Lisa every year?

Women Artists Today

Too many to mention. You may have heard of:

Tracey Emin
Rachel Whiteread
Gillian Wearing
Charlotte Harris

(This doesn't necessarily mean you will want their art in your bedroom!)

Space for self-portrait

JUST PAINTINGS?

Don't be silly.

Edmonia Lewis (1843–c.1900)
Edmonia was the first black woman to be recognized as a sculptor. She made many busts of famous people who fought to end slavery. Edmonia's mother was a Chippewa Indian and her father was African American. The Chippewa called her 'Wildfire'. At college she was accused of trying to poison two white students, and although she was proved innocent, she was not allowed to graduate.

GET THE PICTURE?

Lots of great women artists but not always great opportunities.

The J. Paul Getty Museum,
Los Angeles,
Henry Herschel Hay Cameron,
Julia Margaret Cameron
1874
Albumen silver
Image: 25.4 x 21.4 cm

Know who this is?
Hmmm . . .

Actually she looks a bit miserable.
Let's try something else . . .
That was a picture of Julia Margaret Cameron, but I don't think she was having a good day.

Here is one of her photographs of someone else instead.

The J. Paul Getty Museum,
Los Angeles,
Julia Margaret Cameron,
Ellen Terry at Age Sixteen,
Julia Margaret Cameron
Negative 1864; Printed about 1875
Carbon
Image (round): Diam.: 24.1 cm

Julia Margaret Cameron (1815–1879)

This is a photograph taken by Cameron of the actress Ellen Terry, who was a huge star in British theatre. Julia's daughter gave her a camera when she was 48 and she soon became a brilliant photographer. Hardly anyone had a camera then, so hers were some of the very few pictures we have of famous people like the naturalist Charles Darwin, the writers Alfred Lord Tennyson, Robert Browning and William Michael Rossetti, and the painters John Everett Millais, Edward Burne-Jones and George Frederic Watts.

SNAPPY WOMEN

Antoinette de Correvont

The very first professional woman photographer. She opened her own studio in Munich, Germany, in 1843.

Constance Fox Talbot

William Henry Fox Talbot is known as the 'father of photography'. He became interested in it because he couldn't draw. His wife, Constance, also took, developed and printed photos but her work is often overlooked.

Harriet Tytler (1827–1907)
Robert Tytler is famous for photographing scenes from the Indian Mutiny of 1857. The fact that his wife Harriet worked as his partner is rarely mentioned.

Genevieve-Elizabeth F. Disdéri (1817–1878)
Elizabeth was married to André-Adolphe-Eugène Disdéri, a French photographer known for his *cartes-de-visite* – little photos the size of a visiting card. He ran his business in partnership with Elizabeth; after he died, from 1872 to 1878 she kept up her own Paris studio. Despite this her death certificate read 'without profession, 61 years old'.

Anna Atkins (1799–1871)
The first person ever to print and publish a book with only photographic illustrations. She is buried with her husband in Halstead, Essex. The grave refers to her husband as a Justice of the Peace, but she is simply 'daughter of . . .'

Christina Broom
(1863–1939)
Christina was probably the first British woman press photographer. She photographed women suffragettes demonstrating as early as 1908 and went on to cover all sorts of events, from Derby Day to royal visits and the Oxford and Cambridge boat race.

MUSIC

She looks like a disco diva.

Who is this?
(It's Minerva, of course, goddess of music.)

Who invented music?

The Romans reckoned music was invented by the goddess Minerva, the daughter of Jupiter and Metis. Now, everyone thinks their birth is special, but she was born out of her dad's head and arrived fully armoured and bearing a shield. His headache can only have got worse when she started playing her music. All artists, poets and actors worshipped her and the temple of Minerva in ancient Rome was an important centre of the arts.

Have you heard the story about Adam and Eve and the music?

There is a legend about Adam and Eve that goes like this: one afternoon while Adam was asleep, Eve decided to make some holes in a reed and began playing a tune. Adam woke up and yelled, 'Stop making that horrible noise. If anyone's going to make it, it's me.'

What happened here?

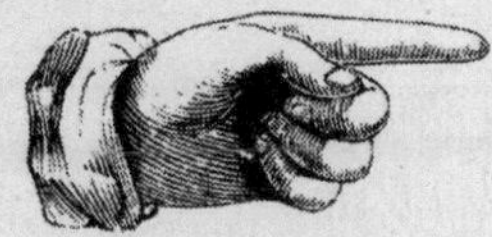

Is this another history lesson?
Yes, it goes right back in history to . . .

2006

The Proms are world-famous concerts held every year at the Royal Albert Hall in London.

Q. Of the 70 or so BBC Prom concerts given at the Albert Hall in 2006, how many included pieces composed by women?

A. It's enough to make you want to be a medieval nun because the answer is . . . .

NONE!

So what's the story?

(as this is the music section, do try and sing the next bit)

For many years women weren't allowed to perform music. They weren't even allowed to sing the female roles in opera until the 18th century! If a woman was any good, lots of things acted against her:

First of all – Women were supposed to get married and stay home with their babies. Both Marianne Mozart and Fanny Mendelssohn could have been great composers but gave up their careers to raise families. In fact Felix Mendelssohn published six of his sister Fanny's songs under his own name.

Second – Only rich women were given a musical education.

Third – If they have a go, patrons, publishers and concert promoters usually didn't want to hire women or publish their music.

Great Women Composers

Marianne Martinez (1744–1812)
Marianne was taught by Haydn and composed over 200 works, including a symphony, concertos, a large oratorio, masses, and lots of keyboard and vocal works. She wrote more large-scale works than any woman composer of past centuries yet she never applied for a job as it 'wasn't done' at the time.

Hildegard of Bingen (1098–1179)
An amazing woman and the first composer in the world whose life story is recorded. She wrote Europe's first opera.

Others:

Anna Amalia
(1739–1807)

Clara Schumann
(1819–1896)

Louise Farrenc
(1804–1875)

Ethel Smyth
(1858–1944)

Joan Tower
(1936–)

Clara Schumann

Ethel Smyth

Child Prodigies

(This is usually quite a dull thing for a kid to be: if you are very clever, no one lets you get on with your games.)

Elisabeth-Claude Jacquet de la Guerre (1665–1729)

Elizabeth was a French child prodigy. When she was just 13 she was described by one critic as 'the marvel of our century'. This period of music was called the Baroque and she was one of the very few women composers of the time. Her collection of harpsichord pieces was one of a very few printed in 17th-century France.

Amy Beach (1867–1944)

Amy was the first successful American female composer of large-scale music. Most of her work was published under the name Mrs H. H. A. Beach – the initials of her husband. Amy was a child prodigy who could sing 40 tunes by the age of one, was able to read at three, and was composing simple waltzes at four. She began proper piano lessons when she was six and must have been noisy to babysit. By the time she was seven she was giving public performances of Handel, Beethoven and Chopin as well as pieces she'd written herself. When she married a doctor much older than her, she agreed to stop performing in public as he didn't like it. After her husband died she went back to performing and toured Europe. There is a famous concert hall in Boston called the Hatch Shell. It has a granite wall with the names of composers like Bach, Handel, Chopin, Debussy and Beethoven inscribed on it. Amy Beach is the only woman composer to be found there.

Music, art, photography . . .
what have we left out?

Silly me. This is a book.

WRITING

Did you know that the first known writer in history was a woman?

(I'm guessing you're not all that surprised.)

Who was she? Why . . .

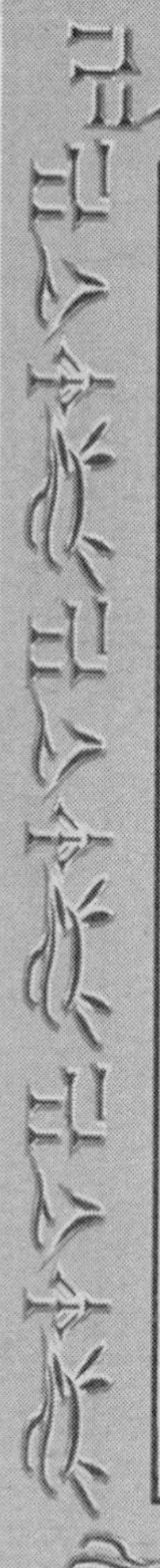

Enheduanna (of course)
(c. 2285–2250 BC)
Ever heard of her? No, she's not big in the shops nowadays. Actually I can't tell you much about her except that she was a woman, probably a princess, and is the world's first known author, male or female. She was writing around 4,300 years ago in something called cuneiform – a series of symbols on a clay tablet. She wrote hymns to the gods, which I'm guessing didn't have a lot of laughs.

More Writing Firsts?

Did you know that Europe's first professional writer was a woman?

Christine de Pizan (1364–1430)
Christine was born in Venice. Her dad worked for Charles V of France and she taught herself in his library. She married young and had three children, but when her husband died she needed to find a way to make money. She started writing love ballads, and between 1393 and 1412 completed more than 300, making her Europe's first professional writer, male or female. She went on to defend women in society and wrote *The Book of the City of Ladies.*

Europe's First Playwright

Hrotsvitha of Gandersheim

(c. 935 to c. 1002)

It won't surprise you to learn that Hrotsvitha was a nun or that there aren't a lot of other Hrotsvithas in history. The ancient Greeks thought that writing plays was a great idea but Hrotsvitha was the first person in the west, boy or girl, who thought so too. She wrote comedies, but they were about good Christian girls and would probably not seem all that funny to us. She was also known as the 'Nightingale of Gandersheim' or the 'Mighty Voice'.

Q. Who invented the game Monopoly?

A. As ever, a man – Charles Darrow – takes the credit, but in fact he based it on a board game devised by Elizabeth Magie.

The world's first novel

The Tale of Genji
was written more than 1,000 years ago by a Japanese woman known as Lady Murasaki ('purple wisteria blossom') . This was a nickname (we don't know her real name). Murasaki was brought up by her father, which was very unusual, and given a boy's education. According to her father, she was very bright, and he was sorry she was a girl. She is considered one of the greatest writers in Japanese literature. Murasaki had a daughter who became a poet.

America's First Black Poet

Phillis Wheatley (1753–1784)

If you think it was tough for white women to get published, imagine being black in the early days of the American colonies. Phillis was the first

Q. Sadly, lots of people in the world can't read. What proportion of them are women?

A. Two-thirds.

African-American female writer to be published in the United States – two years before the American Revolution. Phillis came from Africa as a captured slave when she was seven. In 1761 she was sold to John Wheatley, which is how she got her last name.

Her owners were good people and taught her to read and write. In 1767 Phillis's first poem was published in the *Newport Mercury*; her book of poems appeared in 1773. People found it hard to believe that a black girl could write poems, and John Wheatley had to go to court to prove that she had written them. Her work was published in London because no one in Boston would take it on. After Mr Wheatley died Phillis had a rough time. She died alone in poverty aged 30.

GREAT WOMEN WRITERS

You may not have heard of:

Charlotte Turner Smith
(1749–1806)
but you will probably have heard of Jane Austen, Charles Dickens, William Wordsworth and Samuel Taylor Coleridge. Well, they all gave credit to Charlotte for her influence on their writing. When she was 15, she married Benjamin Smith. The couple were soon in debt and Charlotte began writing to earn money for her children. Her first book was an instant success. She wrote quickly and soon had many novels published. She was hugely popular in her lifetime.

Charles Dickens

But you will definitely have heard of:

Jacqueline Wilson

Jacqueline is one of the most famous writers in Britain. She has sold more than 25 million books in the UK with titles like *The Story of Tracy Beaker*, *Girls Under Pressure* and *The Illustrated Mum*.

So Many Women with Great Stories

Isabella Lucy Bird (1831–1904)
Isabella was born in Yorkshire and grew up to be one of the world's first travel writers. Her dad was a priest so the family moved around Britain wherever he was posted. Isabella always wanted to travel; when she was 23 her dad gave her £100 to go to America. She wrote a book called *The Englishwoman in America* (1856) and lots of people liked it. She went on to travel in Canada, Australia and Hawaii, as well as crossing over 800 miles of the Rocky Mountains riding a horse with a man's saddle. During her time in the mountains she fell in love with an outlaw.

Later she visited Japan, China, Vietnam and Singapore, and, when she was nearly 60, India, Tibet, Persia, Kurdistan and Turkey; she also travelled with the British army between Baghdad and Tehran. In 1892 she became the first woman member of the Royal Geographical Society, a famous club in London for explorers and travellers.

In 1897, when she was 66, she sailed up the Yangtze and Han rivers in China and visited Korea. Later she went to Morocco, where she lived among the Berbers. She was given a black stallion by the sultan; being too short to get onto it, she used a ladder. She died planning another trip.

A very incomplete and impossible list of great women writers:

Jane Austen *(British novelist)*
The Brontë Sisters *(British novelists)*
Louisa May Alcott *(American novelist)*
Margaret Atwood *(Canadian novelist + poet)*
Emily Dickinson *(American poet)*
Zora Neale Hurston *(African-American novelist)*
Li Qingzhao *(Chinese poet)*
Toni Morrison *(African-American novelist)*
Virginia Woolf *(British novelist)*
Aphra Behn *(early British playwright)*
Sappho *(Greek poet)*
Al-Khansa *(Arabian poet)*
Lady Mary Wortley Montagu *(British travel writer)*
Maya Angelou *(African-American poet)*
Huo Xuan Huong *(Vietnamese poet)*
Mary Shelley *(British novelist)*

Jane Austen

Emily Dickinson

Above: A poster advertising Mary Shelley's Frankenstein

Aphra Behn

Lady Mary Wortley Montagu

Heavens, what a lot of CULTURE we've had – art, literature, music. How about something a bit less stressful?

Grab some popcorn

Let's take a break and go to

The Movies

In the early days of the movies, when there was no sound and they were all in black and white, there were plenty of women in charge.

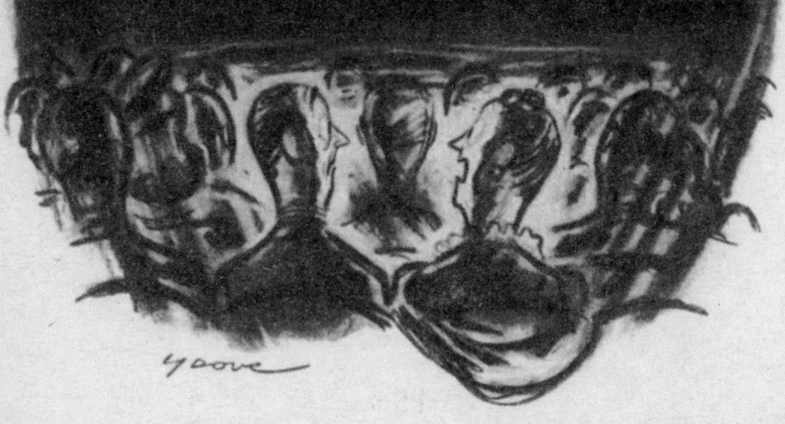

Alice Guy Blache (1873–1968)

Alice was the first woman to direct a film. In 1896 she made *La Fée aux Choux*. She went on to direct about 400 French films and 354 American ones. Most of them were one-reel comedies. In 1912 she became the first woman to have her own studio.

Lois Weber (1881–1939)

In 1914 Lois was the first woman to direct a full-length feature film – *The Merchant of Venice*. Lois ran away from home in Allegheny, Pennsylvania, to become a singer in New York. She was terribly poor and made money singing and preaching on street corners. By 1916 she was Universal Studios' highest-paid director, and in 1917 she formed her own company, Lois Weber Productions. Lois was the first and only woman to be granted membership of the Motion Picture Directors Association.

This is all very well but what about the important stuff like:

BEING IN CHARGE

Good point.
Let's see . . . I know.

About half the people in the world are female. So what is wrong with this picture? *(These people are the leaders of all the countries in the European Union.)*

There is only one woman.

The United Nations has 192 member countries, plus two other independent states who don't belong. Of those 194 countries only 19 have female leaders at the moment.

So you might think boys are best at being in charge, but history teaches us that's not true. As long as there have been groups of people living together there have been powerful female rulers.

MATRIARCHY

When women are in charge of everything in a society, it's called a matriarchy. (When men are in charge it's called business as usual.) There are plenty of matriarchies in the animal kingdom:

Elephants
Ants
Termites
Bison
Killer Whales
Lions
Spotted Hyenas
Bees
Snakes
Bonobos
(a type of chimpanzee)

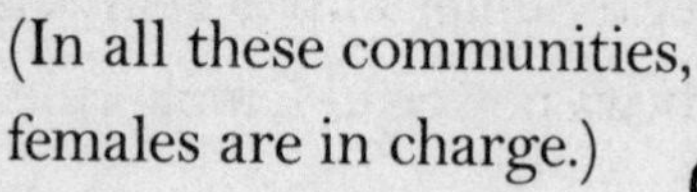

(In all these communities, females are in charge.)

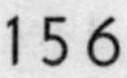

Q. What percentage of countries have no women ministers in their government?

A. 93 per cent.

Ancient People

When we look back, it seems that people in the past had no problem with women being in charge.

The first queen we find mentioned ruled Mesopotamia (that's Iraq, a bit of Iran and a touch of Syria to you and me).

The people were called Sumerians, and in about 2500 BC their queen was:

Kubaba

She was an innkeeper, so she sold drink and probably liked a laugh. She was said to have ruled for 100 years so she must have been very old.

This is a picture of her holding a pomegranate and a mirror. No, I don't know why.

Walk Like an Egyptian

The ancient Egyptians had no problem with women being in charge. Their women could own property, divorce their husbands and be in charge of things; kids traced their family back through their mother's line, not their father's. Of course, they also had rulers like:

Cleopatra (69–30 BC)

Cleo was a pharaoh. In fact she was the last pharaoh of ancient Egypt. That means she was in charge. Her family life must have been a bit confusing because she was the seventh one to be called Cleopatra, and although she ruled Egypt she mostly spoke Greek. Her people believed she was the reincarnation of Isis, the goddess of wisdom.

Hatshepsut (around 1500 BC, even earlier than Cleopatra)

You will have spotted something unusual about Hatshepsut – and I don't just mean that she isn't wearing a top.

The beard?

Before Hatshepsut became Queen of Egypt the Egyptians had only ever had men in charge. She came to the throne because her dad, the king, and both her brothers had died. It was not easy for her because lots of people didn't like the idea of a queen. To overcome some of her problems Hatshepsut dressed like a man so that she looked like the king the people were used to. She even had a false beard.

Despite the beard Hatshepsut was a beautiful woman and very good at getting her own way. Her reign was very peaceful and saw the creation of many beautiful monuments and works of art. When she died in 1458 BC, her nephew tried to remove her name from history. He had her name scrubbed off monuments or, where she was dressed like a man, put a man's name underneath. Against all the odds, Hatshepsut ruled the most powerful and advanced civilization in the world. Her beautiful temple at Deir el-Bahri still stands west of Thebes.

What about the British?

Boudicca

Here's one you've probably heard of. About 2,000 years ago Boudicca was the warrior queen of the Iceni. They lived in Norfolk, in the east of Britain. At that time the Romans were running Britain and Boudicca didn't like it. In AD 60 or 61 she led her people in revolt. They destroyed Camulodunum (Colchester) and got rid of the Roman legion sent to protect the town.

There was more fighting as the Romans abandoned Londinium (London), and Verulamium (St Albans) was burned down. Boudicca was finally defeated in the Battle of Watling Street but not before about 75,000 people had been killed.

Queen Matilda (c.1031–1083)

You hear a lot about William the Conqueror but not much about the woman who was in charge whenever he decided to go off for a spot of conquering. William's wife, Matilda, was only 4'2" tall – probably England's smallest ever queen.

She had ten or eleven children so you might think she would have been rather busy. She didn't always use her power in a nice way, as this story shows: Before she married William she had been in love with the English ambassador to Flanders. His name was Brihtric but he had such pale skin he was nicknamed 'Snow'. Sadly for Matilda, he was already married. Years later, she confiscated Snow's lands without any trial or even proper charges and threw him in prison. He died there – many people thought she'd poisoned him.

There have been wonderful women in charge all over the world.

The Last Hindu Ruler of Kashmir

During its years as a Hindu state, women were treated equally with men in Kashmir (in north-west India). The upper classes were educated and women could own property. Didda, a widowed queen, ruled there for 50 years until AD 1003.

You may read that the last Hindu ruler of Kashmir was a man called Udyan Dev, but actually his wife ran the place. **Queen Kota Rani** (?–1339) appointed the prime minister and the commander-in-chief. When Kashmir was attacked by Tartars, Udyan Dev escaped to Tibet, but Kota Rani rallied the local people to fight back under her banner.

Unfortunately she gave shelter to a Muslim man called Shah Mir Khorasani who, when Udyan Dev died, seized the throne. He tried to make Kota Rani marry him but she killed herself instead. So Hindu rule ended in Kashmir.

Rani Lakshmibai (1828–1858) was such a strong opponent of British rule in India that she is sometimes called the Boudicca of India. Her mother died when she was four, so her father brought her up, teaching her to fence, shoot and ride a horse from a very young age. She became Queen of the state of Jhansi in northern India through her marriage to the maharaja of Jhansi in 1842. They adopted a son, who was called Damodar Rao. The very next day the maharaja died. The British refused to accept Damodar Rao as the maharaja's son and decided to take over the state of Jhansi.

Rani gathered an army which included women and had a lot of popular support. In 1857 she successfully defended Jhansi against the invading armies. Sadly it was taken by the British a few months later and the rani escaped, disguised as a man, with her son tied to her back. She was eventually killed in the battle for Gwalior. The British General Rose said she was 'the bravest and the best' of the rebels.

The Indian National Army's first female regiment was named after her. They fought in Burma during the Second World War.

Yeah, but girl leaders are soft, aren't they?

Well, not always.
There have been quite a few you wouldn't want to mess with.

Empress Dowager Lü (?–180 BC)
Lü was married to Emperor Gao of the Chinese Han dynasty and was famously power mad. She was quick to execute anyone who didn't agree with her. When her husband died, she murdered one of his illegitimate sons, Liu Ruyi, and killed his mother by blinding her and cutting off her limbs.

Emperor Irene (752–803)
Irene was the wife of the Byzantine Emperor Leo IV. When Leo died, their son Constantine VI was only ten so she took over, insisting on being known as Emperor rather than Empress. When Constantine grew up, he wanted to be in charge and tried to push her aside so she had him kidnapped, flogged and his eyes gouged out.

Khadija of the Maldives (?–1380)
The Maldives have had a few women in charge but Khadija was one you wouldn't forget. She probably came to power after murdering her young brother. In 1363 her husband tried to take over so she killed him too. Ten years later her second husband tried the same thing and met a similar fate.

Isabella I of Castile (1451–1504)

Isabella was married to Ferdinand of Aragon. When they were attacked, Isabella put on armour and led her army in the field. She was brilliant at planning, organizing supplies and field hospitals. In 1475, when she was in charge of the army in Toledo, her enemies were allowed a break from fighting only because she had a miscarriage.

Ranavalona I Rabodoandrianampoinimerina of Madagascar (1828–1861)

Ranavalona became Queen when she married Radama, king of the 'Hovas', which sounds like a kind of bread. She wanted to rule alone so she poisoned her husband. Once she was in power she had most of her relatives assassinated.

Queen Supayalat of Burma (1859–1925)

Supayalat is believed to have had about 100 members of her family murdered.

Absolutely nothing to do with anything:

Did you know?

There was once a queen in Bali called **Sakalendukiranaisanagunadharmalakshmidharavijayottunggadevi?**

So women in charge can be tough, ruthless and good at ruling?

Yes.

So, why haven't there been more of them?

The truth?

Taking part in government has not always been easy for women.

For many years in lots of countries women were not allowed to vote and decide who should run their government. This is not ancient history. It was only in 2005 that women in Kuwait were allowed to vote; in Saudi Arabia they are still barred.

British women were only given the same voting rights as men in 1928. In America it was 1920, and in Switzerland 1971!

> **Q.** What percentage of parliamentary seats around the world are held by women?

> **A.** 15 per cent.

Did you know that the first woman to vote in Britain wasn't supposed to?

Lily Maxwell (c.1800–1876)

Lily worked as a maid in Manchester. When she was a widowed, around 1861, she opened a small china shop, which meant she paid rates to the council. In 1867 there was a by-election for the local MP. At the time women were not allowed to vote but all men who paid rates were. Lily's name mistakenly appeared on the list of voters – which caught the eye of Lydia Becker, a 'suffragist' who was fighting for women's votes. She encouraged Lily to use her vote. Lily was rather timid but in the end went to the polls and voted, the first woman ever to do so in Britain. In those days people said their votes out loud and Lily's surprise appearance earned her a round of applause. It seems that she didn't manage to keep her shop; she died in the Union Workhouse, Withington, Manchester.

Lots of brave women fought for the right to vote:

Carrie Burnham Kilgore (1838–1909)
Carrie was a teacher and doctor in America. She got her medical degree in 1865, and in 1883 became the first American woman to be awarded a law degree. It had taken her 11 years to persuade the University of Pennsylvania Law School to accept her. Carrie was determined that women should get the vote. She took her case to court on the grounds that she met the legal

definition of a citizen of the United States. The court did not agree. She also tried to stand for office but was refused permission. Sadly she died before her dream of taking part in democracy came true.

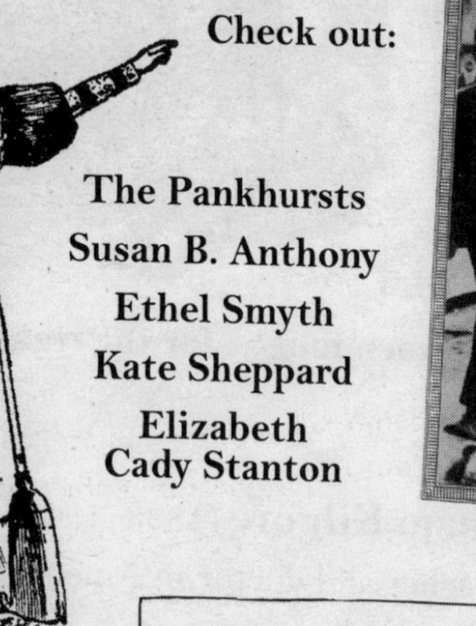

Check out:

The Pankhursts
Susan B. Anthony
Ethel Smyth
Kate Sheppard
Elizabeth Cady Stanton

Mrs Pankhurst

If ever you think you can't be bothered to vote, remember: women died for this right.

The story of one woman and the king's horse:

Emily Davison
(1872–8 June 1913)

Emily went to Oxford University and would have gained a first-class degree – except that they didn't give degrees to women in those days. Emily was committed to the principle of women's 'suffrage' – the right to vote. For the 1911 census, everyone had to state where they were that night. Emily hid overnight in a cupboard in the Palace of Westminster so that she could put 'the House of Commons' as her place of residence.

On 8 June 1913 she went to Epsom racecourse in Surrey, where a famous horse race called the Derby was about to take place. King George V's horse Anmar was running in the race. As the horse galloped along the track, Emily ran out carrying the banner of the women's suffrage movement. She was hit by the horse and killed.

Phew!

Let's take a minute.

I can't help feeling something important and brilliant has been left out. What is it?

Girls Are Best because . . .

Oh, of course . . .

THEY CAN HAVE BABIES!

Did you know that all human beings are basically girls?

For the first six weeks of life, every embryo in the mother's womb looks exactly the same – they all look like girls. Humans have 46 chromosomes, including two sex chromosomes. In girls these are XX and in boys they are XY. Some scientists believe that the basic human being is female and that boys only develop because of one different chromosome. That's why the Y is sometimes called a broken X.

Girls Make Brilliant Parents

In the animal kingdom babies are usually brought up by their mums. Baby animals need milk and only female adults can provide it. Female pigs can have up to 18 teats to suckle their babies.

Some mums may go a bit too far

The Caecilian

The Caecilian probably ought to win the Mum of the Year award. It's a kind of worm that lives underground. When it has babies, it changes some cells so that its skin becomes twice as thick. This is then eaten by its kids. **Ugh!**

LET'S BE HONEST

If you are a boy,
you might think
mentioning the baby
thing was a bit of a
cheat. Of course, girls
are best at having
babies because boys
can't do that . . .

Except for:

Pipefish

These are little fish that look like stretched-out seahorses. With pipefish it is the girls who compete for boys and they often breed with more than one. This is because it's the boys who get pregnant and carry the eggs.

OK, but it's better for boys because they don't have to stay home with the babies getting bored.

Except for:

The Northern Jacana

These are wading birds found in the tropics. They have huge feet and claws so they can walk on anything floating in the shallow lakes where they live. The females are larger than the males, and they leave the males to incubate the eggs while they keep an eye out for predators. One female will often have as many as four males to build a nest and look after her kids.

The Western Barking Frog

This North American dad has a go at parenting. What does he do? He stays near the eggs until they're hatched, keeping them moist by weeing on them. Not much of a dad job, is it?

There must be things girls can't do.

Of course, there must.

Let's see . . .

Bull Fighting?

What about:

Conchita Cintron (1922–?)

Conchita grew up in Lima, Peru. Also known as the 'blonde goddess', she was the first professional woman bullfighter. She started fighting bulls in Mexico in 1937, when she was 15. She fought for 13 years and killed 800 bulls. In those days women were only permitted to fight the bulls on horseback. In 1949 Conchita was in the ring in Jaén in Spain for her last fight. She asked permission of the *presidente* to get off her horse and make the kill on foot. Permission was refused but Conchita did it anyway. She was immediately arrested for breaking the law. The furious audience nearly rioted and she was immediately pardoned. It was said to be one of the most dramatic moments in bullfighting history. The writer and director Orson Welles said about her: 'Her record stands as a rebuke to every man of us who has ever maintained that a woman must lose something of her femininity if she seeks to compete with men.'

Boxing

Hessie Donahue

In 1892 a 'fun' boxing match was staged in a theatre, with Hessie up against legendary heavyweight champion John L. Sullivan. When he accidentally hit her during the act, she knocked him down. Sullivan was out cold for over a minute.

Motorcycling

Adeline (1884–?) and
Augusta Van Buren (1889–?)

In 1916 the Van Buren sisters became the first women to ride motorcycles 5,500 miles across America, from Brooklyn, New York, on 5 July to San Francisco in California on 12 September. On the way they were arrested several times – not for speeding but for wearing men's clothes. They were also the first women to conquer the 14,100-foot Pikes Peak in Colorado on motorcycles.

Horse Riding

Alicia Meynell (1772–?)

In 1804, at the age of 22, Alicia became the first English woman jockey when she took part in a four-mile race in York, riding her boyfriend's horse. She led for three miles. Why didn't she win? She was the only person riding side-saddle.

Ada Evans Dean

In 1906 Ada's horse was entered for a race but on the day her jockey fell ill. Ada rode in two races in Liberty, New York. She won even though she had never ridden in a horse race before.

The Newmarket Town Plate

This race was first run in 1665. It is four miles long and the oldest racing event in Britain. In 1925 Eileen Joel, aged 18 and wearing a cloche hat, raced against four other women and three men on a horse called Hogier. She won by three lengths.

Judy Johnson

Judy was the first woman licensed to be a professional jockey in America. She rode in her first steeplechase in 1943. She had applied to the Maryland Jockey Club for a licence back in 1927 but was turned down on the grounds that no woman had ever had one before. She finally got her licence only because so many men had gone to fight in the war.

Anthea Farrell

In 1991 Anthea became the first girl to beat the boys at the famous Aintree course, when she won the John Hughes Memorial Trophy on J-J-Henry.

Fishing!

If you think fishing is a boys' sport then you don't know about:

Dame Juliana Berners (c. 1450)
Little is known of Lady Juliana except that she was an abbess at a convent near St Albans. She wrote the first known essay on fishing – 'A treatyse of fysshynge wyth an Angle', showing that she couldn't spell but could describe how to make a rod and flies, tell you when to fish, and list the different kinds of fishing.

In 1954 an Australian woman called **B. Byer** caught a 1,052-pound white shark. You should have seen the one that got away . . .

Q. What is the best way to communicate with a fish?

A. Drop it a line.

All right . . .

Shooting!

Annie Oakley (1860–1926)
Annie was incredible with a gun. She was the sharp-shooting star of Buffalo Bill's Wild West Show. She could hit a moving target while riding a galloping horse; hit a small coin in mid-air; and regularly shot a cigarette from her husband's lips.

Did you know that the Olympic rules were changed because one woman is so good at shooting?

Look out for:

Zhang Shan

Zhang Shan is a Chinese sharp-shooter. In the 1992 Olympics she beat 40 men and five women and won the gold medal. Four years later women were barred from competing with the men.

It's not the only time women have been stopped because they were too good.

The Great Baseball Scandal

From 1931 to 1992 women were banned from professional baseball. The reason? One girl was just too good for the boys.

Virne Beatrice 'Jackie' Mitchell (c.1912–1987)
When Jackie was 16 she was a talented pitcher (the one who throws the ball) for a women's team in Chattanooga, Tennessee. A year later a man from the Chattanooga Lookouts, a professional team, offered her a contract for the 1931 season. She was the only woman in the team.

Once a year the Lookouts (who were a very small team) played an exhibition match against the world-famous New York Yankees. Their team included two of the most famous baseball players of all time – Babe Ruth and Lou Gehrig. To strike out a player the pitcher has to stop the batter getting any runs. In front of 4,000 fans Jackie, who was left-handed, struck out both Ruth and Gehrig.

The man in charge of professional baseball, Kenesaw Mountain Landis, heard about it; he was furious and immediately banned women from baseball, saying it was 'too strenuous' for them. Women remained banned from the official game for 60 years.

Women even had problems in the original Greek Olympics

The first Olympics were held in 776 BC in ancient Greece. Women weren't allowed to take part and married women weren't allowed to watch. But they had reckoned without:

Kyniska (born c. 440 BC)
Kyniska was a Spartan princess whose name meant 'puppy'. Spartan women were brought up to play sports and Kyniska was an excellent rider. Her brother thought chariot racing was rubbish, so he persuaded his sister to enter, hoping

everyone would think this kind of racing was unmanly. Kyniska won the four-horse chariot race in 396 BC and again in 392 BC. Despite this, everyone carried on with chariot racing. In the sanctuary of Olympia, an inscription was written declaring Kyniska the only female to win the wreath in the chariot events at the Olympic Games.

Kings of Sparta are my
father and brothers.

Kyniska, conquering with a
chariot of fleet-footed steeds,

Set up this statue. And I
declare myself the only woman

In all Hellas to have
gained this crown.

However, she was not allowed to collect her prize in person.

Marathon Running

When the Olympics were revived in Athens in 1896, women were still banned. This didn't stop:

Melpomene

In 1896 a Greek woman, possibly called Stamata Revithi, wanted to run the marathon. Although banned, she ran the same course as the men, finishing in four hours 30 minutes. She was nicknamed Melpomene after the Muse of Tragedy. Baron Pierre de Coubertin, founder of the modern Olympics, said, 'It is indecent that the spectators

Melpomene

should be exposed to the risk of seeing the body of a women being smashed before their very eyes. Besides, no matter how toughened a sportswoman may be, her organism is not cut out to sustain certain shocks.'

Things took a long time to get better:

K. (Katherine) Switzer

In 1967 Katherine registered to run the Boston Marathon as K. Switzer. When officials realized she was a woman, they tried to tear her number from her back during the race.

Women were finally allowed to race in their own Olympic marathon in 1984.

Here's a funny thing

The Royal and Ancient Golf Club of St Andrews

The Royal and Ancient is one of the world's oldest golf clubs. It is the club that sets the rules for golf. Women are not allowed to be members. Prince Andrew is the captain of the R & A. He got the job because he is the second son of the Queen of England, yet he is captain of a club that she is not allowed to join.

The Royal Musselburgh Golf Club, Scotland

On 9 January 1811 the town's fishwives got together at Musselburgh Golf Club for the first known women's golf tournament.

Juli Inkster

In 1990 Juli won the Invitational Pro-Am at Pebble Beach, California. It's the only professional golf tournament in the world where women and men compete head-to-head.

Heavens – Look at the Time!

We haven't even touched on all the Great Women Scientists

Did you know that **Beatrix Potter**, as well as writing about Peter Rabbit, was an expert on fungi and the first person to identify lichen as a fungus rather than a plant? (I realize you may not care, but I thought I'd mention it anyway!)

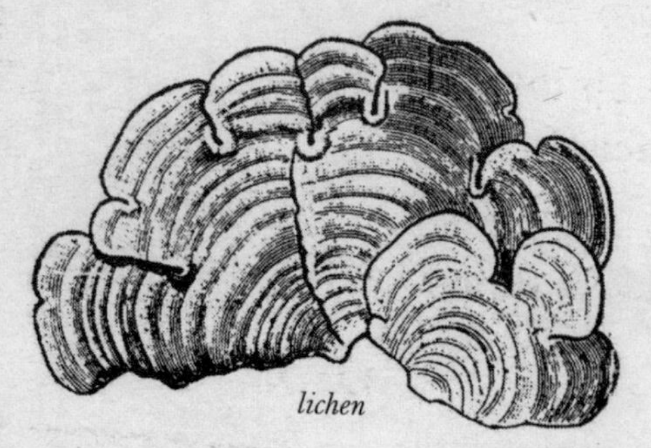

lichen

Check out these

Great Women:

Astronomers (e.g. **Sophia Brahe**)

Mathematicians (e.g. **Hypatia**)

Mountaineers (e.g. **Junko Tabei**)

Architects (e.g. **Zaha Hadid**)

Lawyers (e.g. **Helena Kennedy**)

Teachers (e.g. **Maria Montessori**)

Lighthouse Keepers
(check out **Ida Lewis**)

Explorers (e.g. **Sakajawea**, who guided the great Lewis & Clark expedition with a new baby on her back)

Trade Unionists
(e.g. **Ellen Cicely Wilkinson**)

Peace Activists
(e.g. **Bertha Felicie Sophie Von Suttner**)

Etc., etc., etc., etc. . . .

Girls can be:

CRAZY

Annie Taylor (1855–1921)

In 1901 Annie was the first person ever to go over Niagara Falls in a barrel and survive. She was 43 and couldn't swim. When she was taken out of the barrel after her fall, she said, 'Nobody ever ought to do that again.'

BRAVE

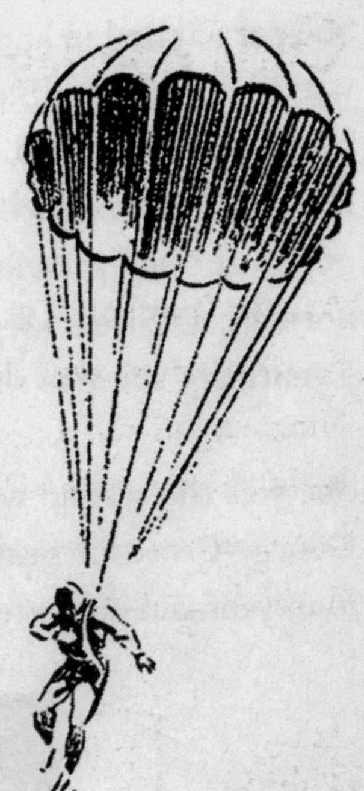

Georgia 'Tiny' Broadwick (1893–1978)
In 1914 Tiny became the first person ever to perform an intentional free-fall parachute jump from an aeroplane. She did it for the US army. Maybe the boys were too scared.

DARING

Violette Szabo (1921–1945)
During the Second World War some brave people worked as secret agents for the British SOE (Special Operations Executive). Violette was said to be their best shot, male or female. When her husband was killed in the war, Violette volunteered for duty in occupied France. Her second mission took place just before D-Day.

She parachuted in and got caught in a gun battle with the Germans. She kept firing her sten gun until she had run out of ammunition and one of the French resistance leaders had managed to get away. Violette was captured, interrogated and horribly tortured but gave away no information. Eventually she was shot.

She was the second woman to be awarded the George Cross for bravery. The king gave it to her four-year-old daughter after her death.

KIND

Catherine (Kitty) Wilkinson
(1786–1860)

Kitty was brought up in Liverpool by her widowed Irish mum. When she was 11, she was sent to work in a cotton textile mill for the next seven years of her life. Kitty married and had two sons, but after her husband died she was left to look after her mentally ill mother and young boys on very little money. She married again but then began to devote her life to the poor and to orphans.

In 1932 there was a cholera epidemic in Liverpool. Kitty tended the sick and offered her kitchen for use as a wash-house where bedding could be washed and disinfected with chloride of lime. This was so successful that, with some financial help, she kept it open after the epidemic was over. A friend of Kitty's sold the idea to the city council, and in 1842 they opened the first public wash-house. It was such a success that the idea spread across Britain. Kitty became so famous that in 1846 the queen gave her a silver tea service. There is a stained-glass window portrait of Kitty in Liverpool Cathedral.

Don't forget – it's not all history. There are amazing girls and women around today.

SPORT

Laura Robson In 2008 Laura became the first British winner of a Wimbledon title in 24 years. She was just 14 when she won the Girls' championship, making her the youngest player in any event at that year's Wimbledon.

Dara Torres From the youngest to one of the oldest. Aged 41, Dara was part of the American swim team at the 2008 Olympics, her fifth Olympic games.

Dame Ellen MacArthur

A sailor who in 2005 broke the world record for the fastest solo circumnavigation of the globe. She was immediately made a Dame.

Lorena Ochoa The first Mexican golfer of either sex to be number one in the world.

SCIENCE

Dr Linda B. Buck In 2004 she received the Nobel Prize for medicine for her work on our sense of smell.

Dame Nancy Rothwell A British neuroscientist doing amazing work on brain injuries.

Dame Jocelyn Bell Burnell An Irish astrophysicist who discovered radiopulsars.

Mary Lou Jepsen An engineer who developed a solar-powered laptop for kids in the developing world.

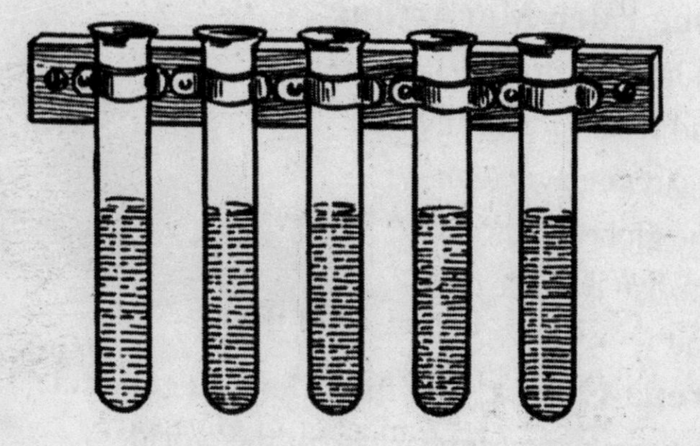

POLITICS

Hillary Clinton Although she didn't win the race to be the Democratic candidate for American president, Hillary Clinton has paved the way for a woman to one day be in charge in the White House.

Aung San Suu Kyi Although she won the election as leader in Burma in 1990, the army won't let her take charge. They keep her under house arrest.

Dr Wangari Muta Maathai A Kenyan environmental and political activist who in 2004 became the first African woman to receive the Nobel Peace Prize for her contribution to sustainable development, democracy and peace.

Michelle Bachelet Current President of Chile.

Sonia Gandhi President of the Indian National Congress.

Angela Merkel Chancellor of Germany.

BUSINESS

Dame Clara Furse
is the Chief Executive of the London Stock Exchange. She was the first woman to be in charge and is regarded as one of the most influential people in the world.

Indra Nooyi
Chairman and CEO of PepsiCo, the fourth-largest food and drink company in the world.

Margaret Whitman
Chief Executive, President of eBay. One of only ten self-made female billionaires on the planet

Wu Xiaoling
Deputy Governor, People's Bank of China.
A powerful woman in a huge economy.

ENTERTAINMENT

Kylie Minogue

Kylie has sold more than 60 million records.

Madonna

The most successful female in UK singles chart history, more UK number one singles than any other female solo artist and, in 2008, she beat Elvis Presley's record as the artist with most top ten hits in the history of the American singles chart.

Oprah Winfrey

Although she is a talk show host some people claim she is the most influential woman in the world. She is the world's only black billionaire.

CHARITY

Dr Carrie Herbert Dr Herbert set up Red Balloon, a charity which helps kids who have been bullied in school to get back to their education.

Camila Batmanghelidjh Camila set up Kid's Company in 1996 to help inner-city kids in London. In 2007 they worked with 12,000 youngsters.

Melinda Gates Co-founder of the Bill and Melinda Gates Foundation, the largest private foundation in the world. They have about US $34.6 billion and give money away to help improve health care and reduce poverty.

Here are a few final questions:

Q. Has this book left some girls out?

A. Thousands and thousands.

Q. Does girls being best mean boys are rubbish?

A. Absolutely not. History has just sometimes forgotten how great girls are.

Q. How do you know I haven't made some mistakes in this book?

A. You don't: I've checked everything out as best I can, but you know, even girls can get things wrong sometimes!

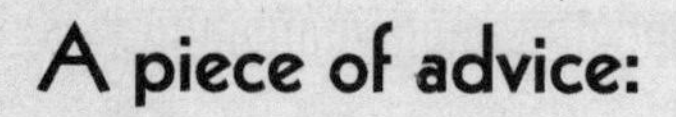
A piece of advice:

If you don't
agree with
something you
have read -
write a book
of your own.